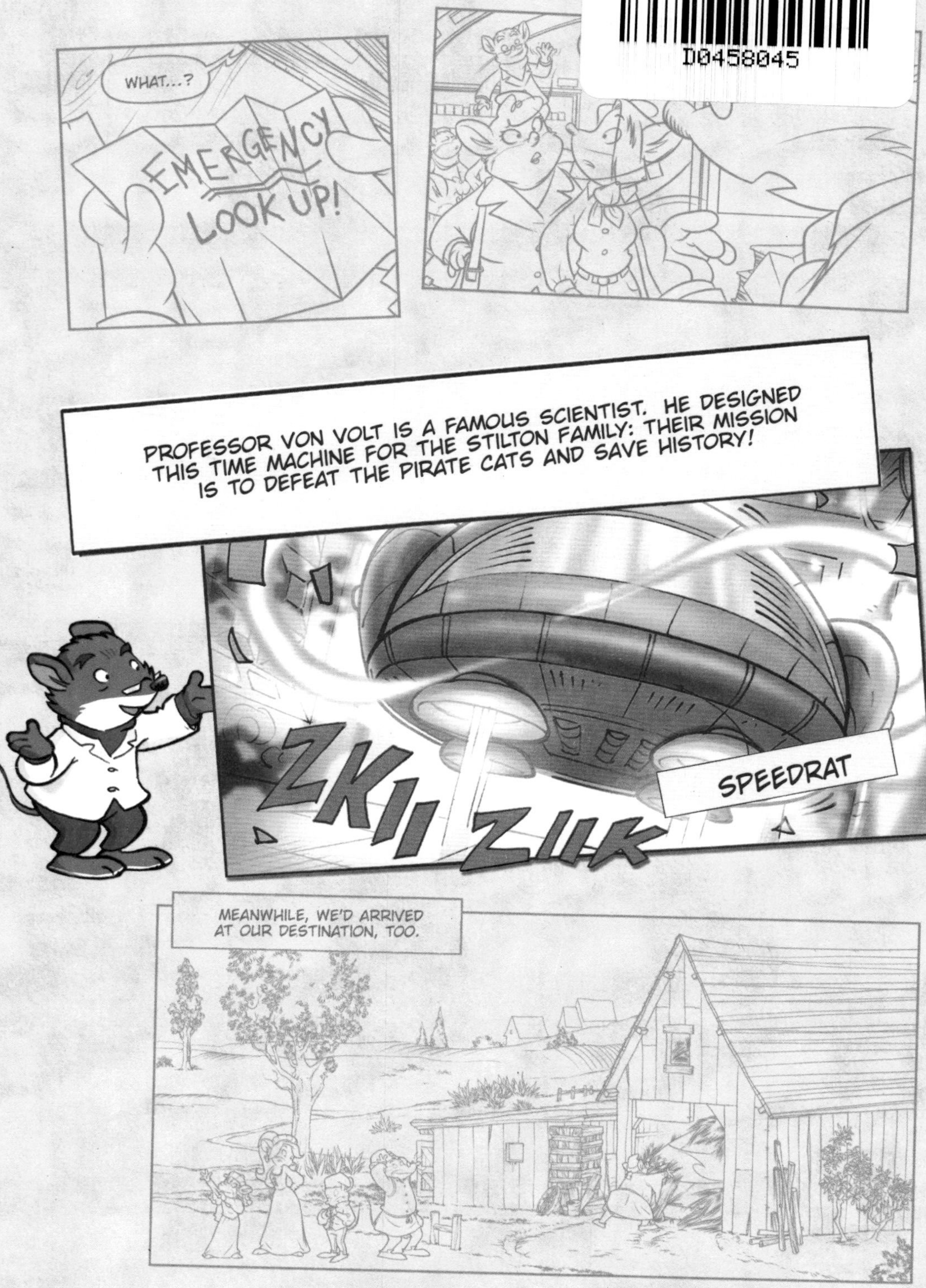
WHAT...?
EMERGENCY LOOK UP!
PROFESSOR VON VOLT IS A FAMOUS SCIENTIST. HE DESIGNED THIS TIME MACHINE FOR THE STILTON FAMILY: THEIR MISSION IS TO DEFEAT THE PIRATE CATS AND SAVE HISTORY!
ZKII ZIIK
SPEEDRAT
MEANWHILE, WE'D ARRIVED AT OUR DESTINATION, TOO.

Geronimo Stilton

THE WEIRD
BOOK MACHINE

PAPERCUT Z ™

Geronimo Stilton

Geronimo Stilton

THE WEIRD
BOOK MACHINE

By Geronimo Stilton

PAPERCUT Z™
New York

THE WEIRD BOOK MACHINE
© EDIZIONI PIEMME 2011 S.p.A.
Tiziano 32, 20145,
Milan, Italy

Text by Geronimo Stilton
Editorial coordination by Patrizia Puricelli
Script by Michele Foschini
Artistic coordination by BAO Publishing
Illustrations by Ennio Bufi and color by Mirka Andolfo
Cover by Marta Lorini
Based on an original idea by Elisabetta Dami

Original title: "Geronimo Stilton La Strana Macchina dei Libri"

Translation by: Nanette McGuinness

www.geronimostilton.com

Lettering and Production by Ortho
Michael Petranek – Associate Editor
Jim Salicrup
Editor-in-Chief

ISBN: 978-1-59707-295-3

Papercutz books maye be purchased for business or promtional use.
For information on bulk purchases please contact Macmillan Corporate and
Premium Sales Department at (800) 221-7945 x5442.

Printed in India
October 2019

Distributed by Macmillan
Sixth Papercutz Printing

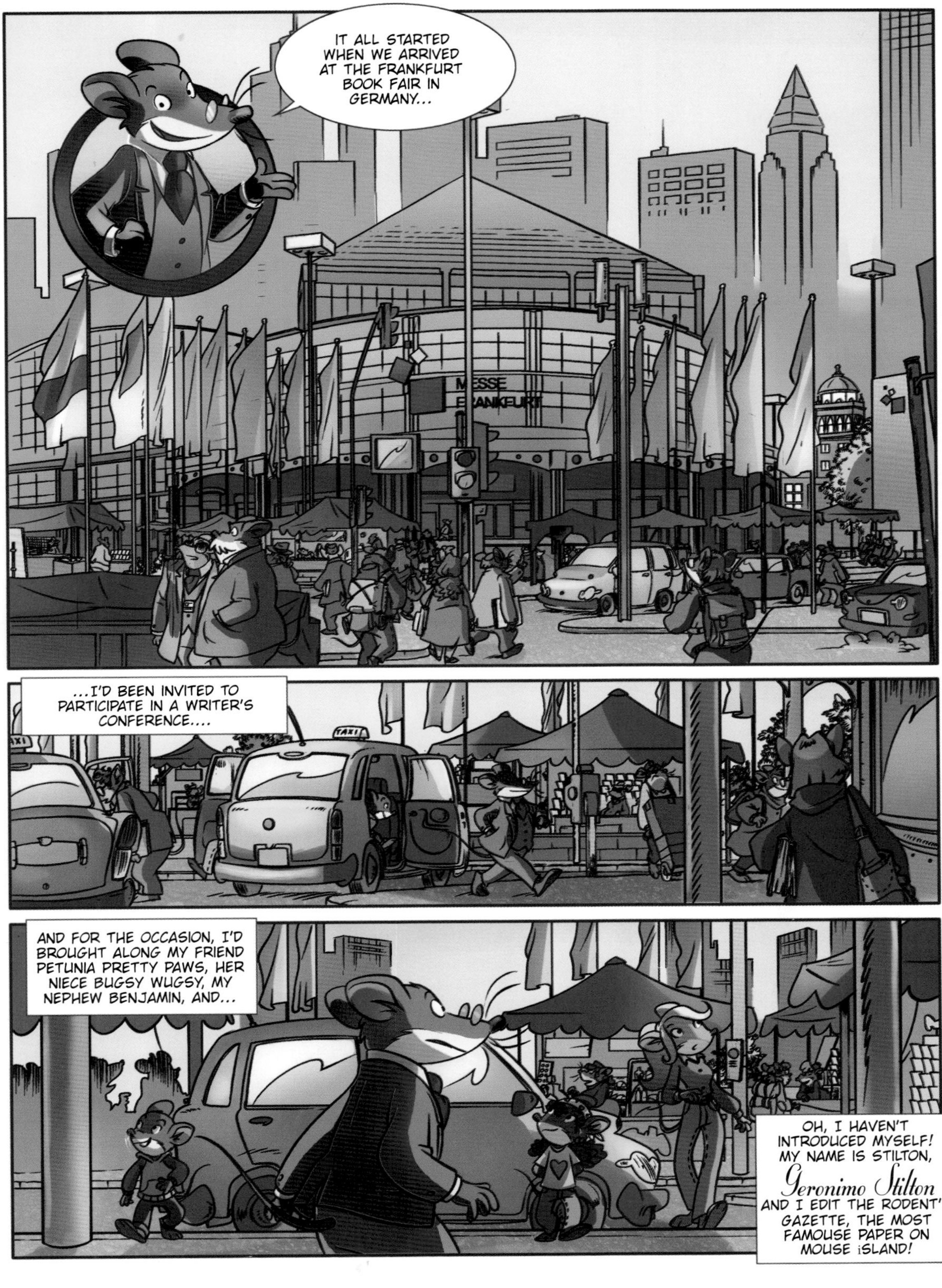
IT ALL STARTED WHEN WE ARRIVED AT THE FRANKFURT BOOK FAIR IN GERMANY...
MESSE FRANKFURT
...I'D BEEN INVITED TO PARTICIPATE IN A WRITER'S CONFERENCE....
TAXI
AND FOR THE OCCASION, I'D BROUGHT ALONG MY FRIEND PETUNIA PRETTY PAWS, HER NIECE BUGSY WUGSY, MY NEPHEW BENJAMIN, AND...
OH, I HAVEN'T INTRODUCED MYSELF! MY NAME IS STILTON, Geronimo Stilton AND I EDIT THE RODENT'S GAZETTE, THE MOST FAMOUSE PAPER ON MOUSE iSLAND!

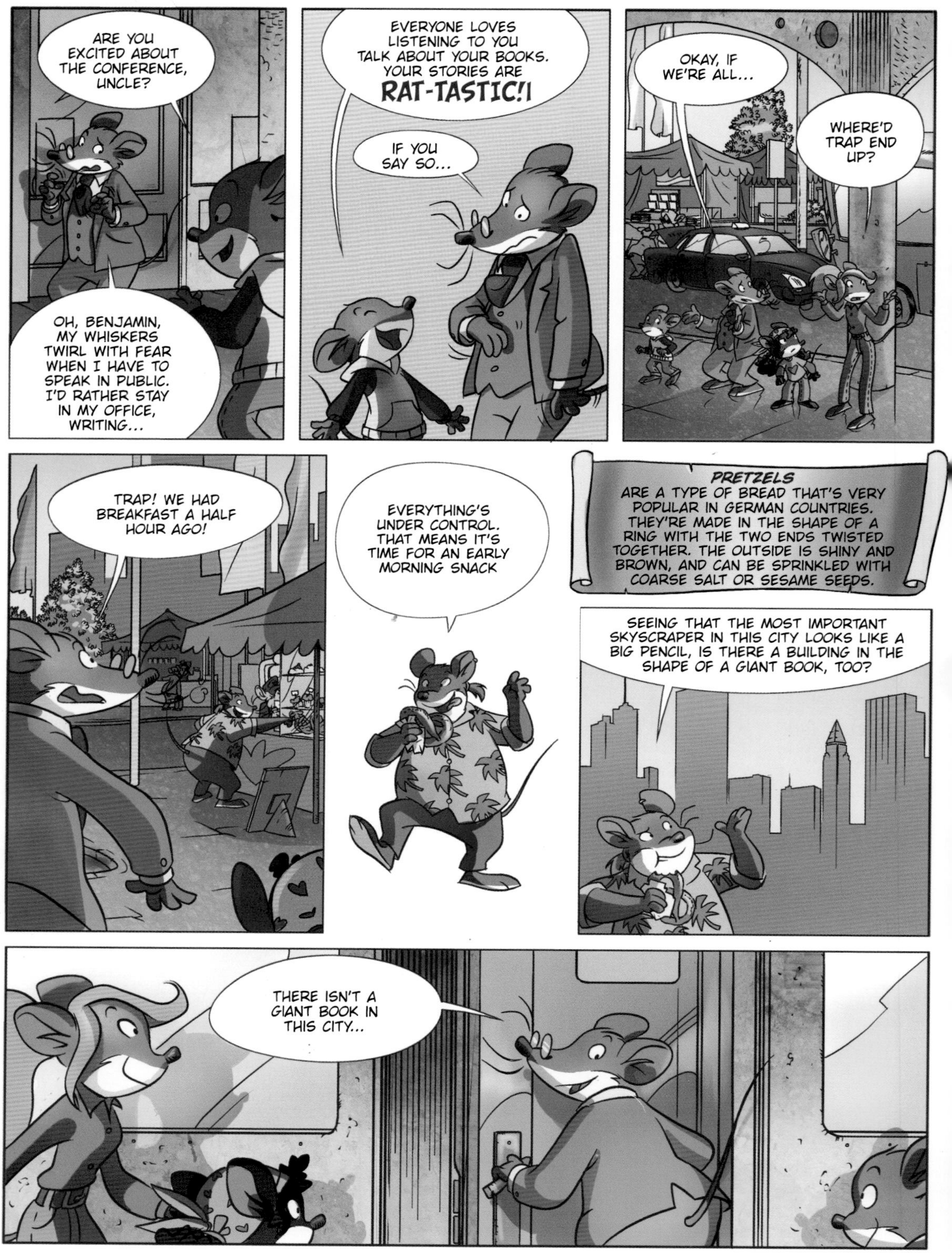
ARE YOU EXCITED ABOUT THE CONFERENCE, UNCLE?
OH, BENJAMIN, MY WHISKERS TWIRL WITH FEAR WHEN I HAVE TO SPEAK IN PUBLIC. I'D RATHER STAY IN MY OFFICE, WRITING...
EVERYONE LOVES LISTENING TO YOU TALK ABOUT YOUR BOOKS. YOUR STORIES ARE RAT-TASTIC!
IF YOU SAY SO...
OKAY, IF WE'RE ALL...
WHERE'D TRAP END UP?
TRAP! WE HAD BREAKFAST A HALF HOUR AGO!
EVERYTHING'S UNDER CONTROL. THAT MEANS IT'S TIME FOR AN EARLY MORNING SNACK
PRETZELS
ARE A TYPE OF BREAD THAT'S VERY POPULAR IN GERMAN COUNTRIES. THEY'RE MADE IN THE SHAPE OF A RING WITH THE TWO ENDS TWISTED TOGETHER. THE OUTSIDE IS SHINY AND BROWN, AND CAN BE SPRINKLED WITH COARSE SALT OR SESAME SEEDS.
SEEING THAT THE MOST IMPORTANT SKYSCRAPER IN THIS CITY LOOKS LIKE A BIG PENCIL, IS THERE A BUILDING IN THE SHAPE OF A GIANT BOOK, TOO?
THERE ISN'T A GIANT BOOK IN THIS CITY...

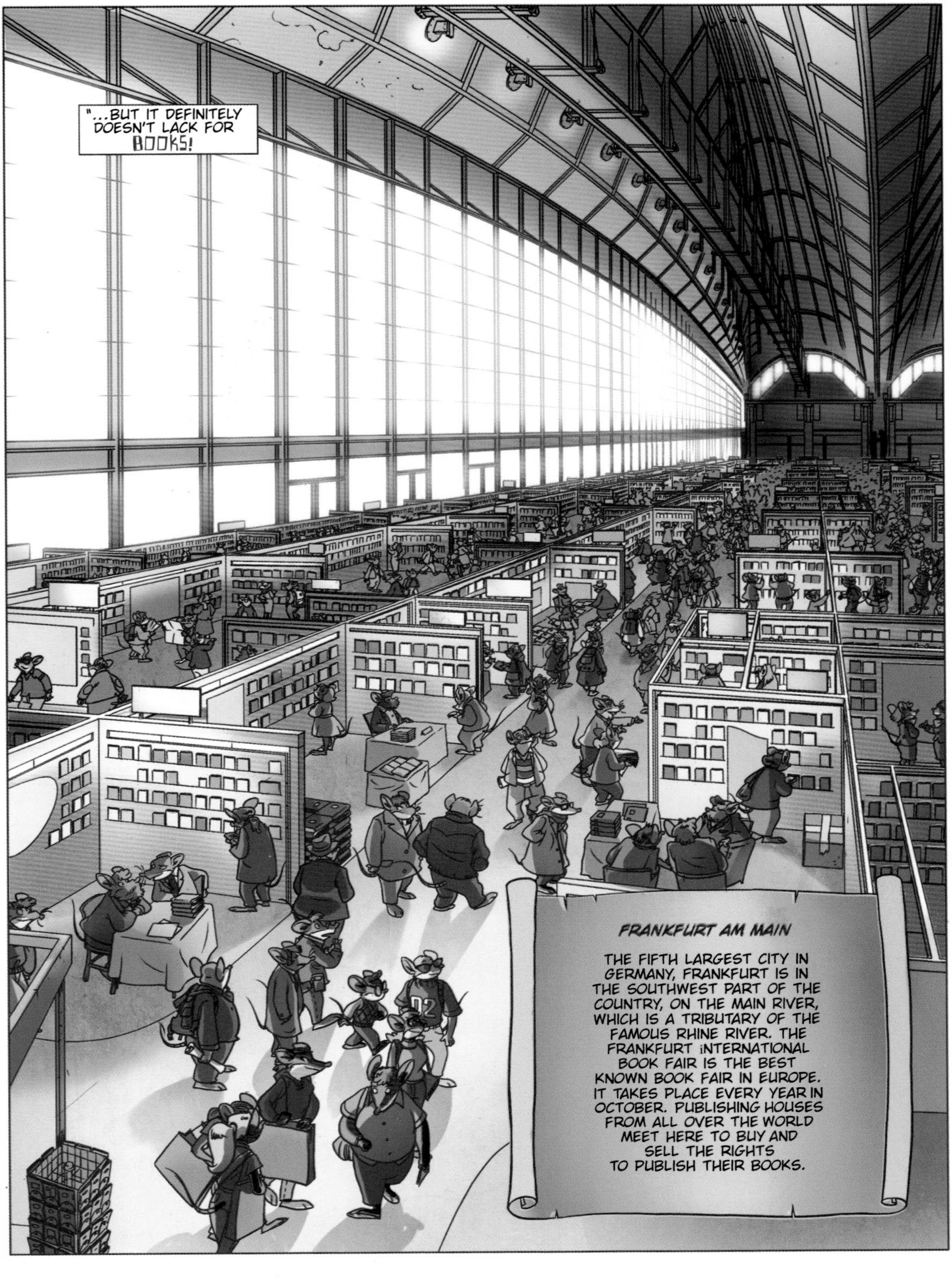
"...BUT IT DEFINITELY DOESN'T LACK FOR BOOKS!
FRANKFURT AM MAIN
THE FIFTH LARGEST CITY IN GERMANY, FRANKFURT IS IN THE SOUTHWEST PART OF THE COUNTRY, ON THE MAIN RIVER, WHICH IS A TRIBUTARY OF THE FAMOUS RHINE RIVER. THE FRANKFURT INTERNATIONAL BOOK FAIR IS THE BEST KNOWN BOOK FAIR IN EUROPE. IT TAKES PLACE EVERY YEAR IN OCTOBER. PUBLISHING HOUSES FROM ALL OVER THE WORLD MEET HERE TO BUY AND SELL THE RIGHTS TO PUBLISH THEIR BOOKS.

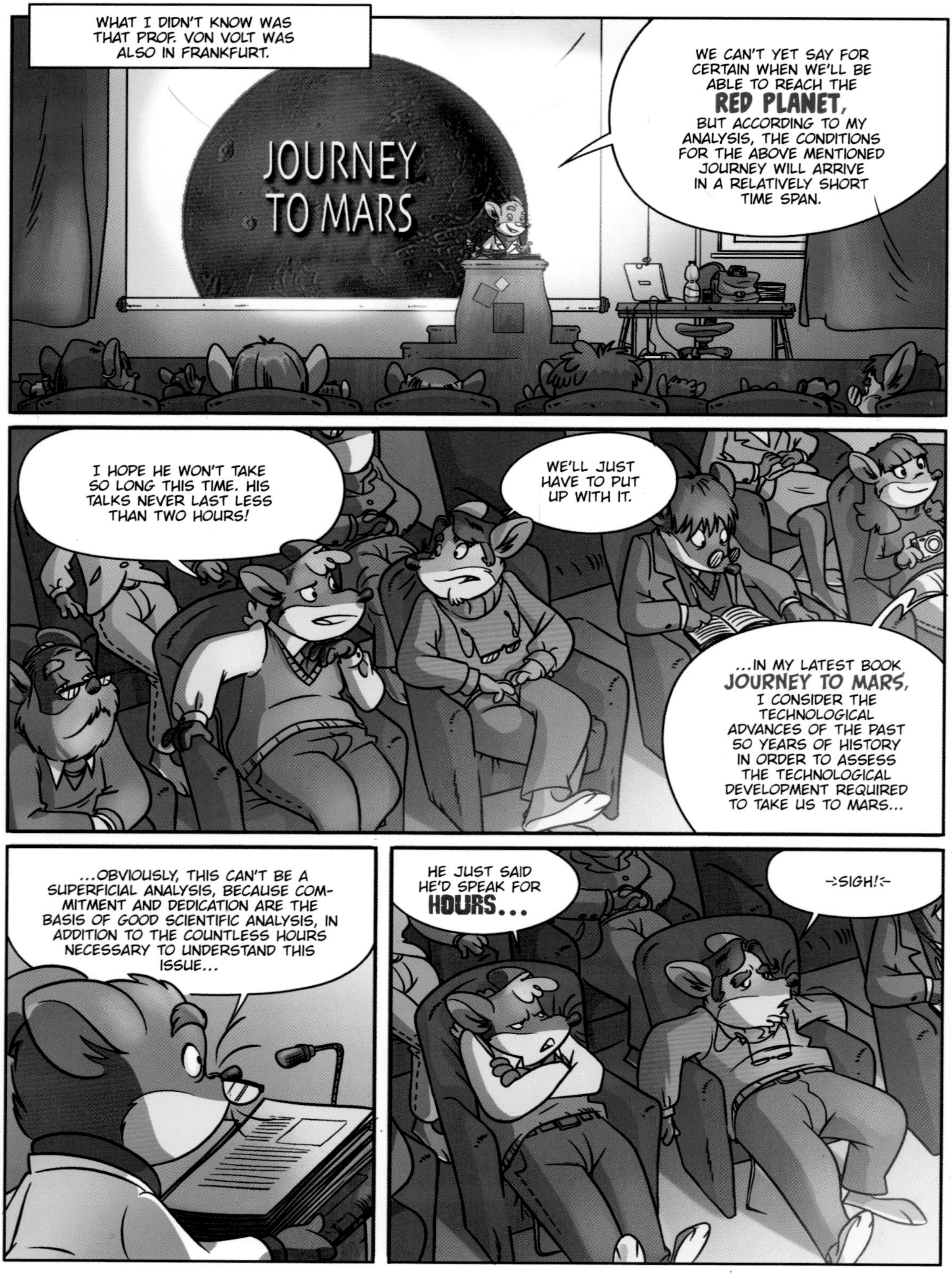
WHAT I DIDN'T KNOW WAS THAT PROF. VON VOLT WAS ALSO IN FRANKFURT.
JOURNEY TO MARS
WE CAN'T YET SAY FOR CERTAIN WHEN WE'LL BE ABLE TO REACH THE RED PLANET, BUT ACCORDING TO MY ANALYSIS, THE CONDITIONS FOR THE ABOVE MENTIONED JOURNEY WILL ARRIVE IN A RELATIVELY SHORT TIME SPAN.
I HOPE HE WON'T TAKE SO LONG THIS TIME. HIS TALKS NEVER LAST LESS THAN TWO HOURS!
WE'LL JUST HAVE TO PUT UP WITH IT.
...IN MY LATEST BOOK JOURNEY TO MARS, I CONSIDER THE TECHNOLOGICAL ADVANCES OF THE PAST 50 YEARS OF HISTORY IN ORDER TO ASSESS THE TECHNOLOGICAL DEVELOPMENT REQUIRED TO TAKE US TO MARS...
...OBVIOUSLY, THIS CAN'T BE A SUPERFICIAL ANALYSIS, BECAUSE COM-MITMENT AND DEDICATION ARE THE BASIS OF GOOD SCIENTIFIC ANALYSIS, IN ADDITION TO THE COUNTLESS HOURS NECESSARY TO UNDERSTAND THIS ISSUE...
HE JUST SAID HE'D SPEAK FOR HOURS...
-SIGH!-

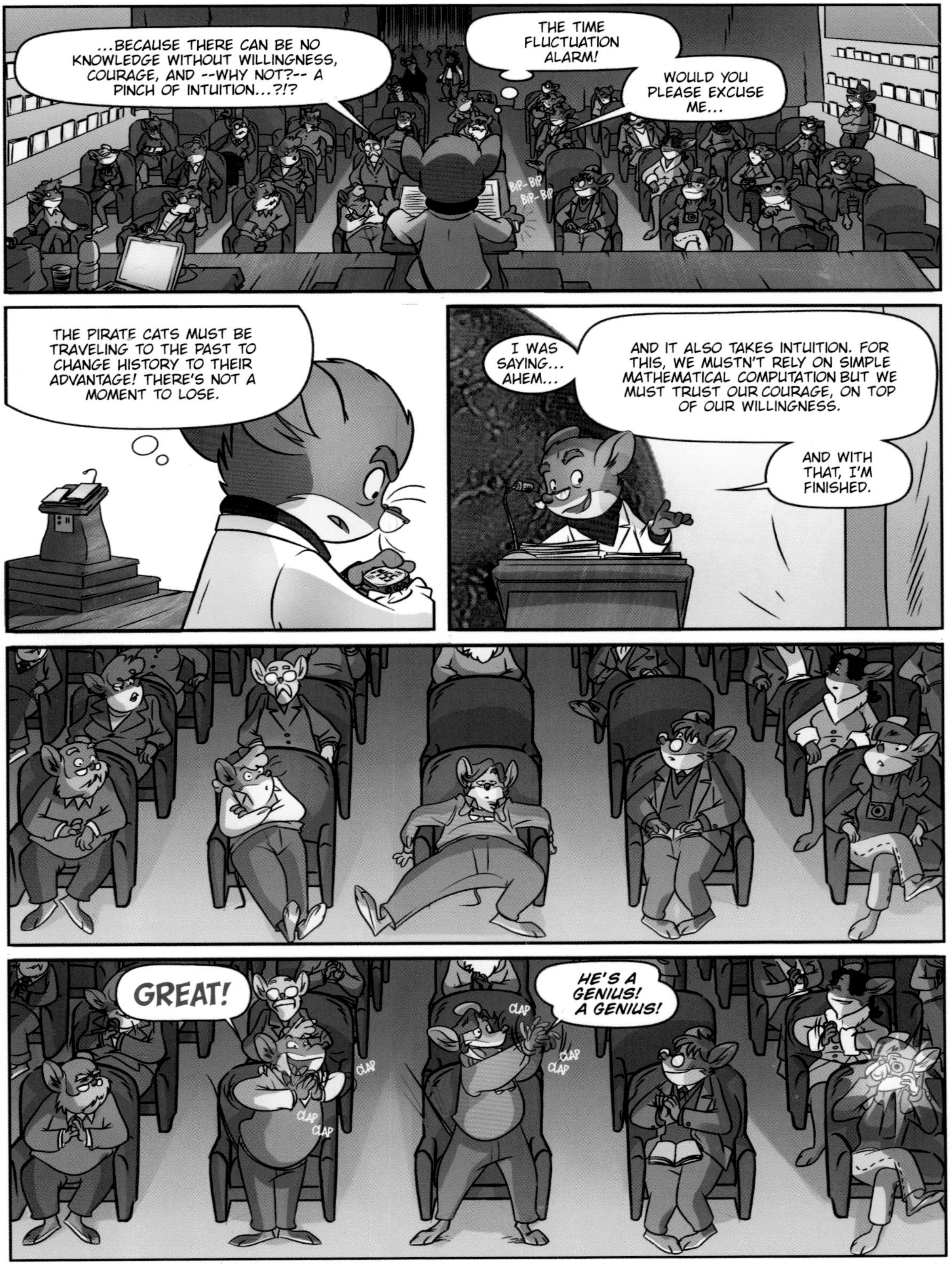
...BECAUSE THERE CAN BE NO KNOWLEDGE WITHOUT WILLINGNESS, COURAGE, AND --WHY NOT?-- A PINCH OF INTUITION...?!?
THE TIME FLUCTUATION ALARM!
WOULD YOU PLEASE EXCUSE ME...
BIP-BIP BIP-BIP
THE PIRATE CATS MUST BE TRAVELING TO THE PAST TO CHANGE HISTORY TO THEIR ADVANTAGE! THERE'S NOT A MOMENT TO LOSE.
I WAS SAYING... AHEM...
AND IT ALSO TAKES INTUITION. FOR THIS, WE MUSTN'T RELY ON SIMPLE MATHEMATICAL COMPUTATION BUT WE MUST TRUST OUR COURAGE, ON TOP OF OUR WILLINGNESS.
AND WITH THAT, I'M FINISHED.
GREAT!
HE'S A GENIUS! A GENIUS!
CLAP CLAP CLAP CLAP CLAP CLAP

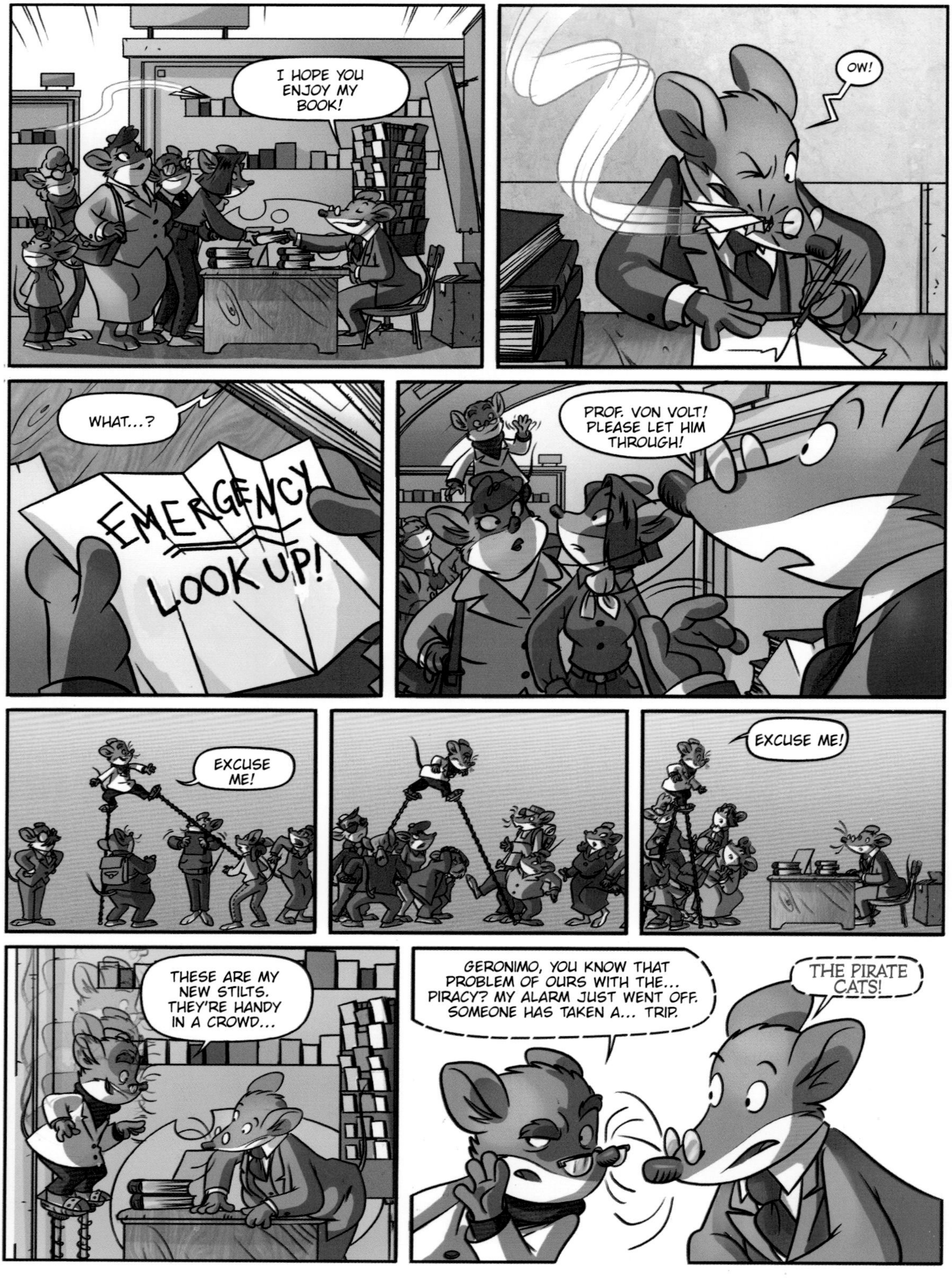
I HOPE YOU ENJOY MY BOOK!
OW!
WHAT...?
EMERGENCY
LOOK UP!
PROF. VON VOLT! PLEASE LET HIM THROUGH!
EXCUSE ME!
EXCUSE ME!
THESE ARE MY NEW STILTS. THEY'RE HANDY IN A CROWD...
GERONIMO, YOU KNOW THAT PROBLEM OF OURS WITH THE... PIRACY? MY ALARM JUST WENT OFF. SOMEONE HAS TAKEN A... TRIP.
THE PIRATE CATS!

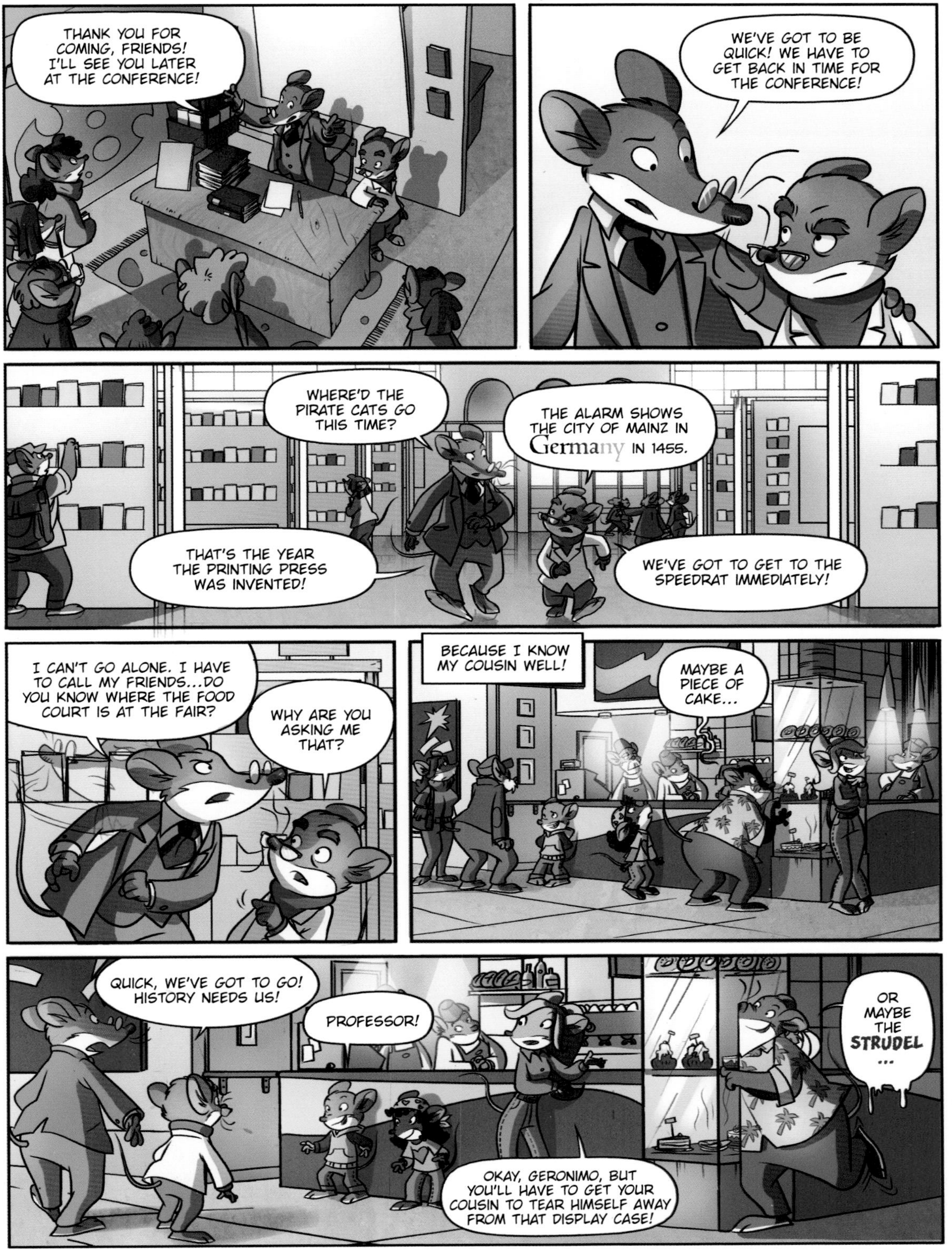
THANK YOU FOR COMING, FRIENDS! I'LL SEE YOU LATER AT THE CONFERENCE!
WE'VE GOT TO BE QUICK! WE HAVE TO GET BACK IN TIME FOR THE CONFERENCE!
WHERE'D THE PIRATE CATS GO THIS TIME?
THE ALARM SHOWS THE CITY OF MAINZ IN Germany IN 1455.
THAT'S THE YEAR THE PRINTING PRESS WAS INVENTED!
WE'VE GOT TO GET TO THE SPEEDRAT IMMEDIATELY!
I CAN'T GO ALONE. I HAVE TO CALL MY FRIENDS...DO YOU KNOW WHERE THE FOOD COURT IS AT THE FAIR?
WHY ARE YOU ASKING ME THAT?
BECAUSE I KNOW MY COUSIN WELL!
MAYBE A PIECE OF CAKE...
QUICK, WE'VE GOT TO GO! HISTORY NEEDS US!
PROFESSOR!
OR MAYBE THE STRUDEL ...
OKAY, GERONIMO, BUT YOU'LL HAVE TO GET YOUR COUSIN TO TEAR HIMSELF AWAY FROM THAT DISPLAY CASE!

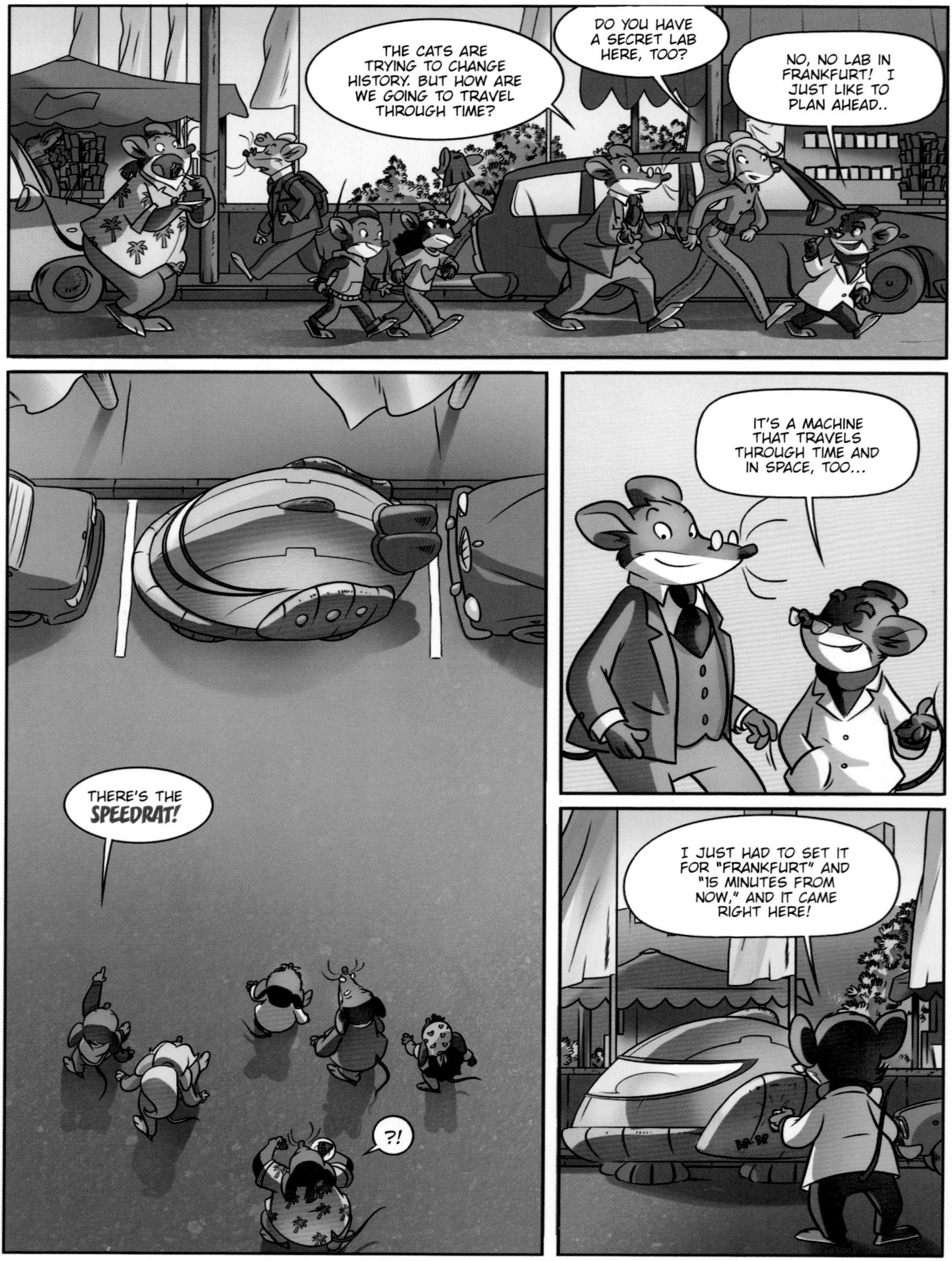
THE CATS ARE TRYING TO CHANGE HISTORY. BUT HOW ARE WE GOING TO TRAVEL THROUGH TIME?
DO YOU HAVE A SECRET LAB HERE, TOO?
NO, NO LAB IN FRANKFURT! I JUST LIKE TO PLAN AHEAD..
THERE'S THE SPEEDRAT!
?!
IT'S A MACHINE THAT TRAVELS THROUGH TIME AND IN SPACE, TOO...
I JUST HAD TO SET IT FOR "FRANKFURT" AND "15 MINUTES FROM NOW," AND IT CAME RIGHT HERE!
BIP BIP

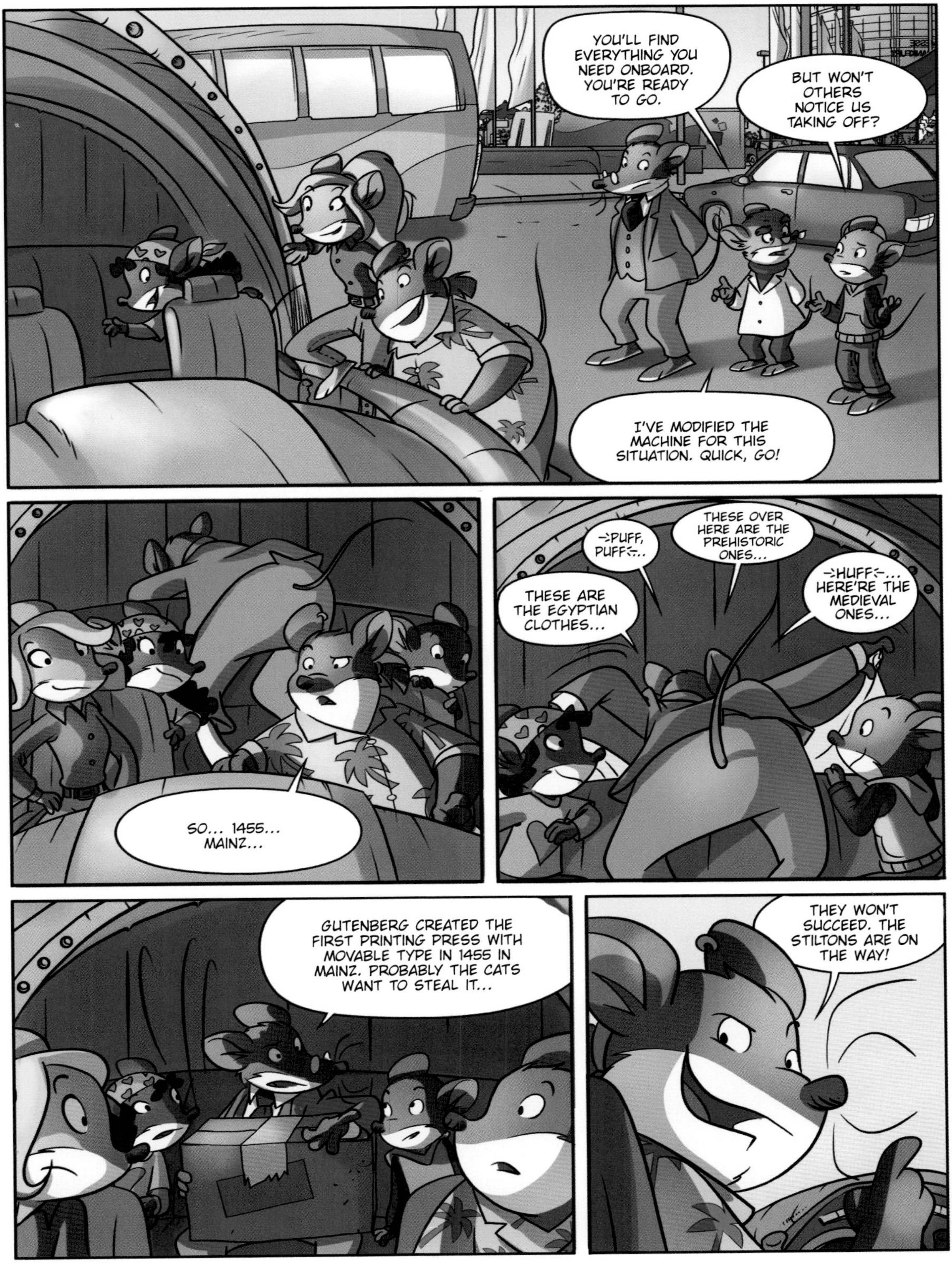
YOU'LL FIND EVERYTHING YOU NEED ONBOARD. YOU'RE READY TO GO.
BUT WON'T OTHERS NOTICE US TAKING OFF?
I'VE MODIFIED THE MACHINE FOR THIS SITUATION. QUICK, GO!
SO... 1455... MAINZ...
THESE ARE THE EGYPTIAN CLOTHES...
->PUFF, PUFF<-...
THESE OVER HERE ARE THE PREHISTORIC ONES...
->HUFF<-... HERE'RE THE MEDIEVAL ONES...
GUTENBERG CREATED THE FIRST PRINTING PRESS WITH MOVABLE TYPE IN 1455 IN MAINZ. PROBABLY THE CATS WANT TO STEAL IT...
THEY WON'T SUCCEED. THE STILTONS ARE ON THE WAY!

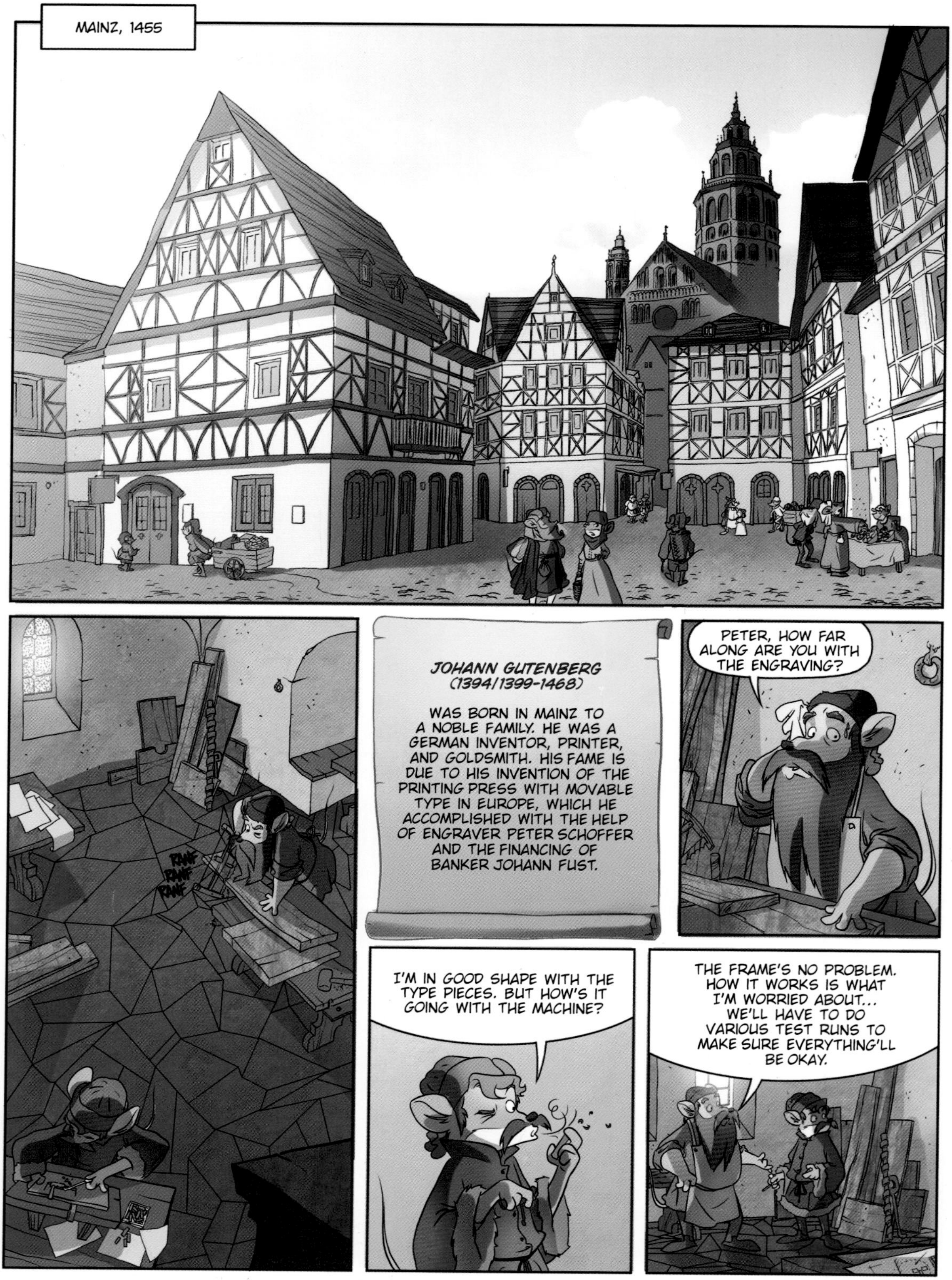
MAINZ, 1455
RANF RANF RANF
JOHANN GUTENBERG (1394/1399-1468)
WAS BORN IN MAINZ TO A NOBLE FAMILY. HE WAS A GERMAN INVENTOR, PRINTER, AND GOLDSMITH. HIS FAME IS DUE TO HIS INVENTION OF THE PRINTING PRESS WITH MOVABLE TYPE IN EUROPE, WHICH HE ACCOMPLISHED WITH THE HELP OF ENGRAVER PETER SCHOFFER AND THE FINANCING OF BANKER JOHANN FUST.
PETER, HOW FAR ALONG ARE YOU WITH THE ENGRAVING?
I'M IN GOOD SHAPE WITH THE TYPE PIECES. BUT HOW'S IT GOING WITH THE MACHINE?
THE FRAME'S NO PROBLEM. HOW IT WORKS IS WHAT I'M WORRIED ABOUT... WE'LL HAVE TO DO VARIOUS TEST RUNS TO MAKE SURE EVERYTHING'LL BE OKAY.

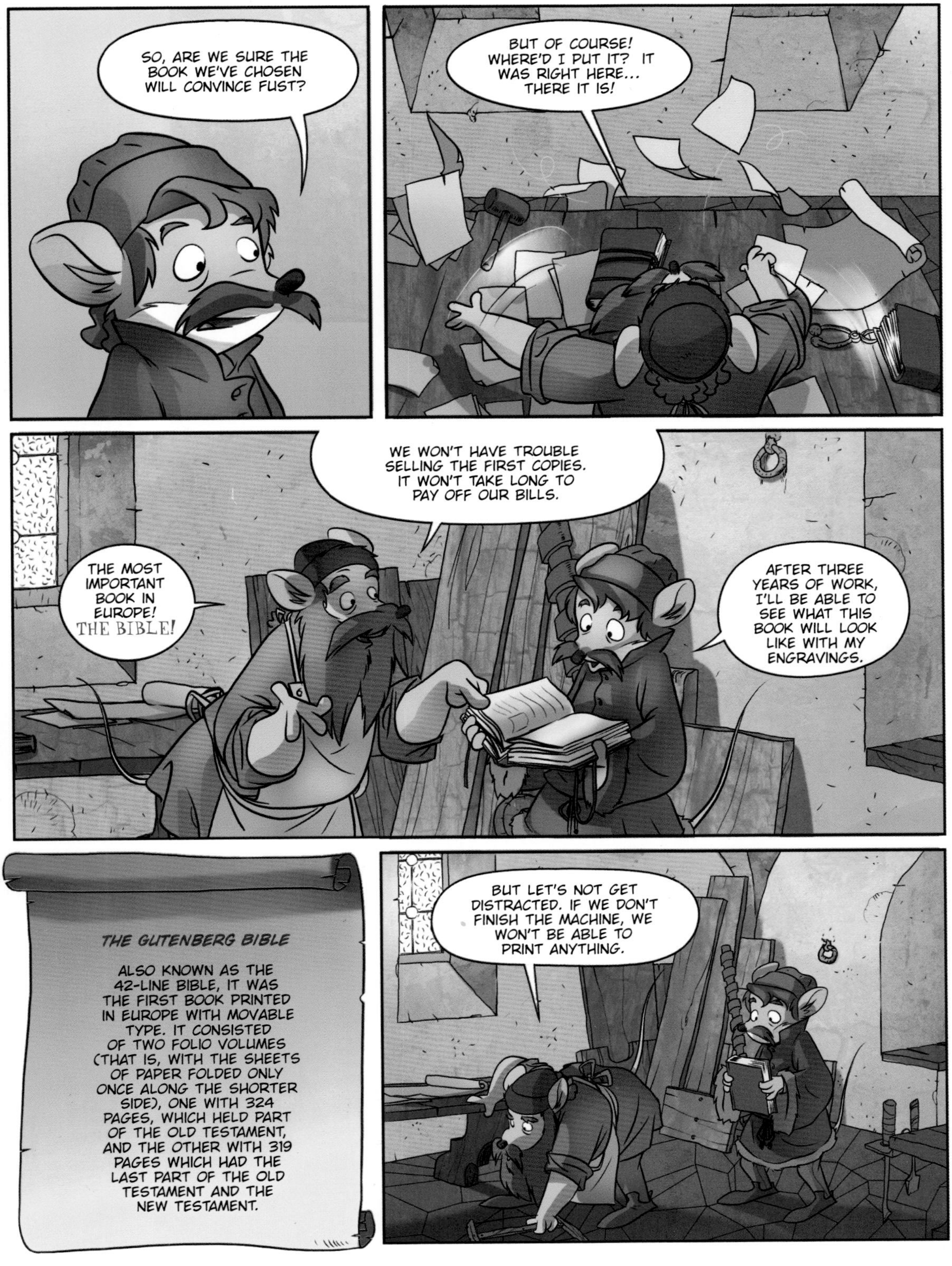
SO, ARE WE SURE THE BOOK WE'VE CHOSEN WILL CONVINCE FUST?
BUT OF COURSE! WHERE'D I PUT IT? IT WAS RIGHT HERE... THERE IT IS!
THE MOST IMPORTANT BOOK IN EUROPE! THE BIBLE!
WE WON'T HAVE TROUBLE SELLING THE FIRST COPIES. IT WON'T TAKE LONG TO PAY OFF OUR BILLS.
AFTER THREE YEARS OF WORK, I'LL BE ABLE TO SEE WHAT THIS BOOK WILL LOOK LIKE WITH MY ENGRAVINGS.
THE GUTENBERG BIBLE
ALSO KNOWN AS THE 42-LINE BIBLE, IT WAS THE FIRST BOOK PRINTED IN EUROPE WITH MOVABLE TYPE. IT CONSISTED OF TWO FOLIO VOLUMES (THAT IS, WITH THE SHEETS OF PAPER FOLDED ONLY ONCE ALONG THE SHORTER SIDE), ONE WITH 324 PAGES, WHICH HELD PART OF THE OLD TESTAMENT, AND THE OTHER WITH 319 PAGES WHICH HAD THE LAST PART OF THE OLD TESTAMENT AND THE NEW TESTAMENT.
BUT LET'S NOT GET DISTRACTED. IF WE DON'T FINISH THE MACHINE, WE WON'T BE ABLE TO PRINT ANYTHING.

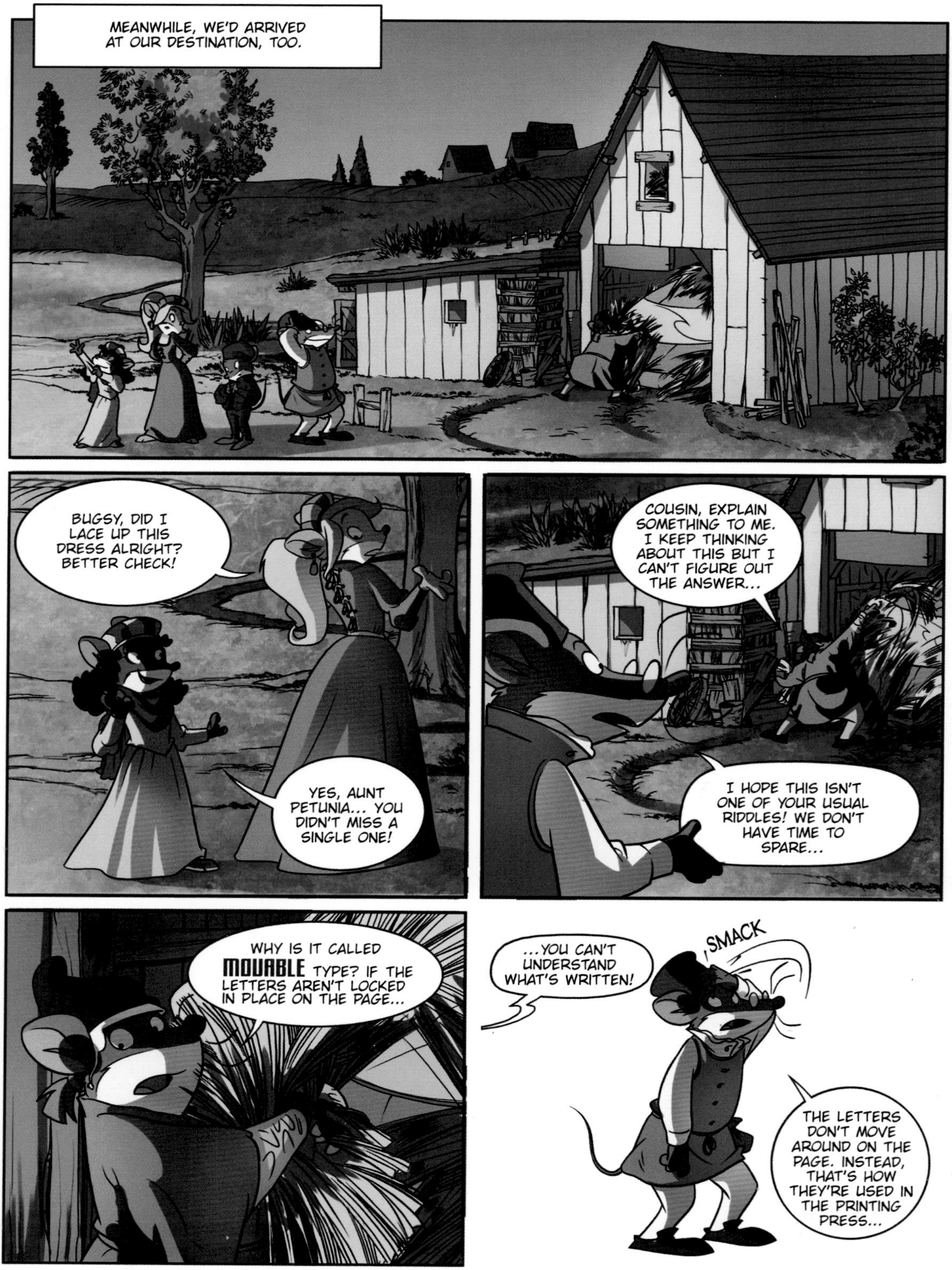
MEANWHILE, WE'D ARRIVED AT OUR DESTINATION, TOO.
BUGSY, DID I LACE UP THIS DRESS ALRIGHT? BETTER CHECK!
YES, AUNT PETUNIA... YOU DIDN'T MISS A SINGLE ONE!
COUSIN, EXPLAIN SOMETHING TO ME. I KEEP THINKING ABOUT THIS BUT I CAN'T FIGURE OUT THE ANSWER...
I HOPE THIS ISN'T ONE OF YOUR USUAL RIDDLES! WE DON'T HAVE TIME TO SPARE...
WHY IS IT CALLED MOVABLE TYPE? IF THE LETTERS AREN'T LOCKED IN PLACE ON THE PAGE...
...YOU CAN'T UNDERSTAND WHAT'S WRITTEN!
SMACK
THE LETTERS DON'T MOVE AROUND ON THE PAGE. INSTEAD, THAT'S HOW THEY'RE USED IN THE PRINTING PRESS...

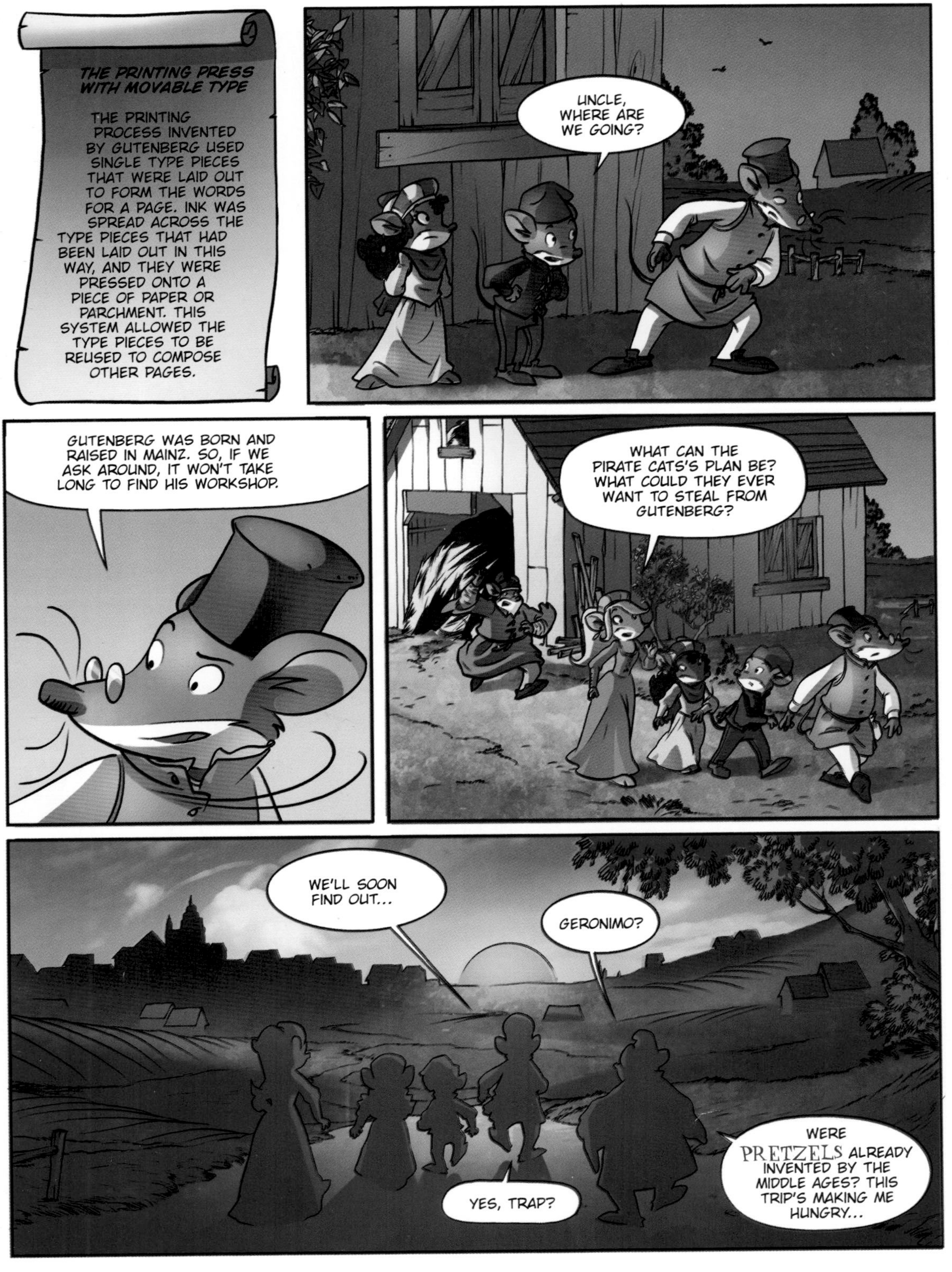
THE PRINTING PRESS WITH MOVABLE TYPE
THE PRINTING PROCESS INVENTED BY GUTENBERG USED SINGLE TYPE PIECES THAT WERE LAID OUT TO FORM THE WORDS FOR A PAGE. INK WAS SPREAD ACROSS THE TYPE PIECES THAT HAD BEEN LAID OUT IN THIS WAY, AND THEY WERE PRESSED ONTO A PIECE OF PAPER OR PARCHMENT. THIS SYSTEM ALLOWED THE TYPE PIECES TO BE REUSED TO COMPOSE OTHER PAGES.
UNCLE, WHERE ARE WE GOING?
GUTENBERG WAS BORN AND RAISED IN MAINZ. SO, IF WE ASK AROUND, IT WON'T TAKE LONG TO FIND HIS WORKSHOP.
WHAT CAN THE PIRATE CATS'S PLAN BE? WHAT COULD THEY EVER WANT TO STEAL FROM GUTENBERG?
WE'LL SOON FIND OUT...
GERONIMO?
YES, TRAP?
WERE PRETZELS ALREADY INVENTED BY THE MIDDLE AGES? THIS TRIP'S MAKING ME HUNGRY...

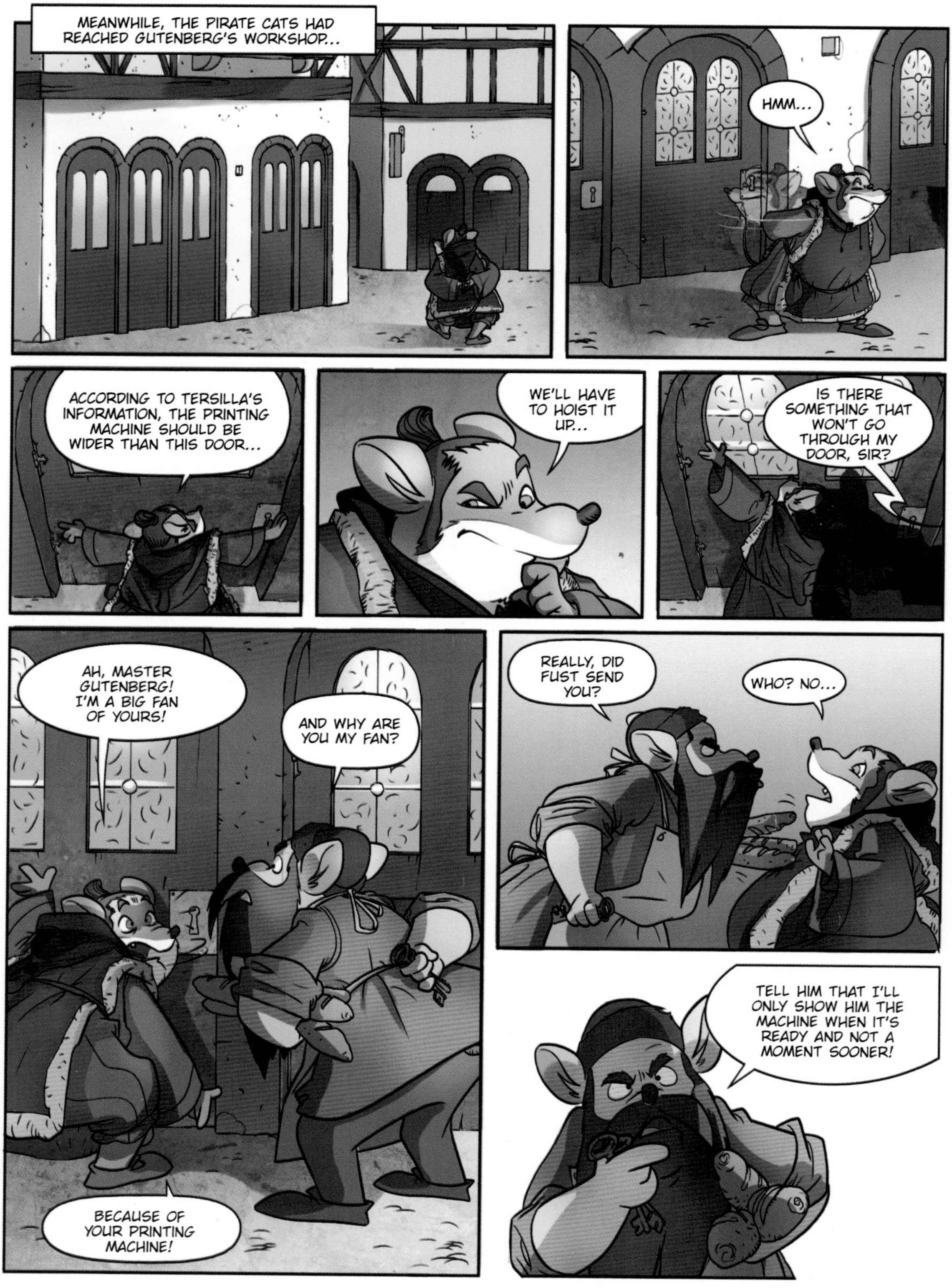

MEANWHILE, THE PIRATE CATS HAD REACHED GUTENBERG'S WORKSHOP...
HMM...
ACCORDING TO TERSILLA'S INFORMATION, THE PRINTING MACHINE SHOULD BE WIDER THAN THIS DOOR...
WE'LL HAVE TO HOIST IT UP...
IS THERE SOMETHING THAT WON'T GO THROUGH MY DOOR, SIR?
AH, MASTER GUTENBERG! I'M A BIG FAN OF YOURS!
AND WHY ARE YOU MY FAN?
BECAUSE OF YOUR PRINTING MACHINE!
REALLY, DID FUST SEND YOU?
WHO? NO...
TELL HIM THAT I'LL ONLY SHOW HIM THE MACHINE WHEN IT'S READY AND NOT A MOMENT SOONER!

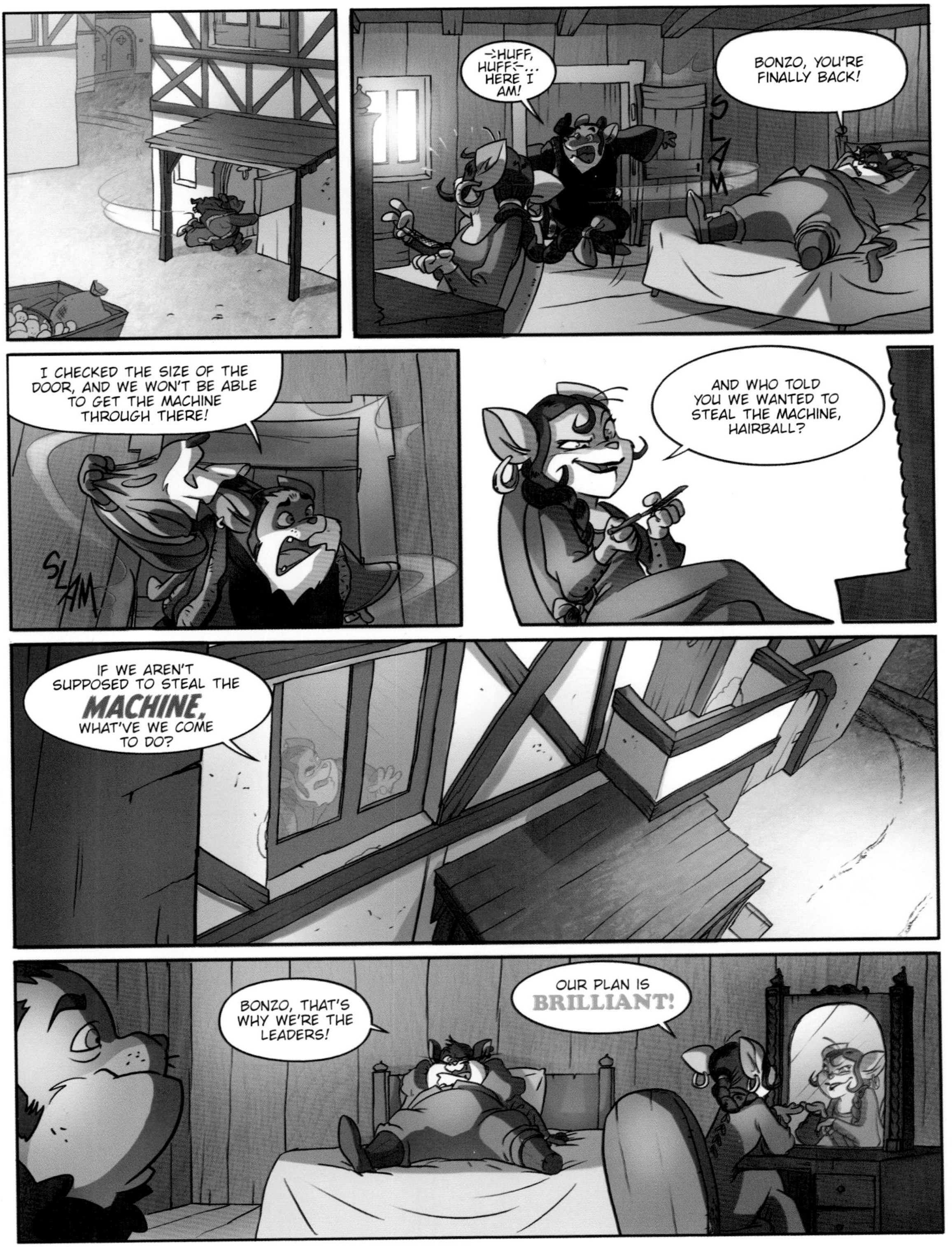
HUFF, HUFF... HERE I AM!
SLAM
BONZO, YOU'RE FINALLY BACK!
I CHECKED THE SIZE OF THE DOOR, AND WE WON'T BE ABLE TO GET THE MACHINE THROUGH THERE!
SLAM
AND WHO TOLD YOU WE WANTED TO STEAL THE MACHINE, HAIRBALL?
IF WE AREN'T SUPPOSED TO STEAL THE MACHINE, WHAT'VE WE COME TO DO?
BONZO, THAT'S WHY WE'RE THE LEADERS!
OUR PLAN IS BRILLIANT!

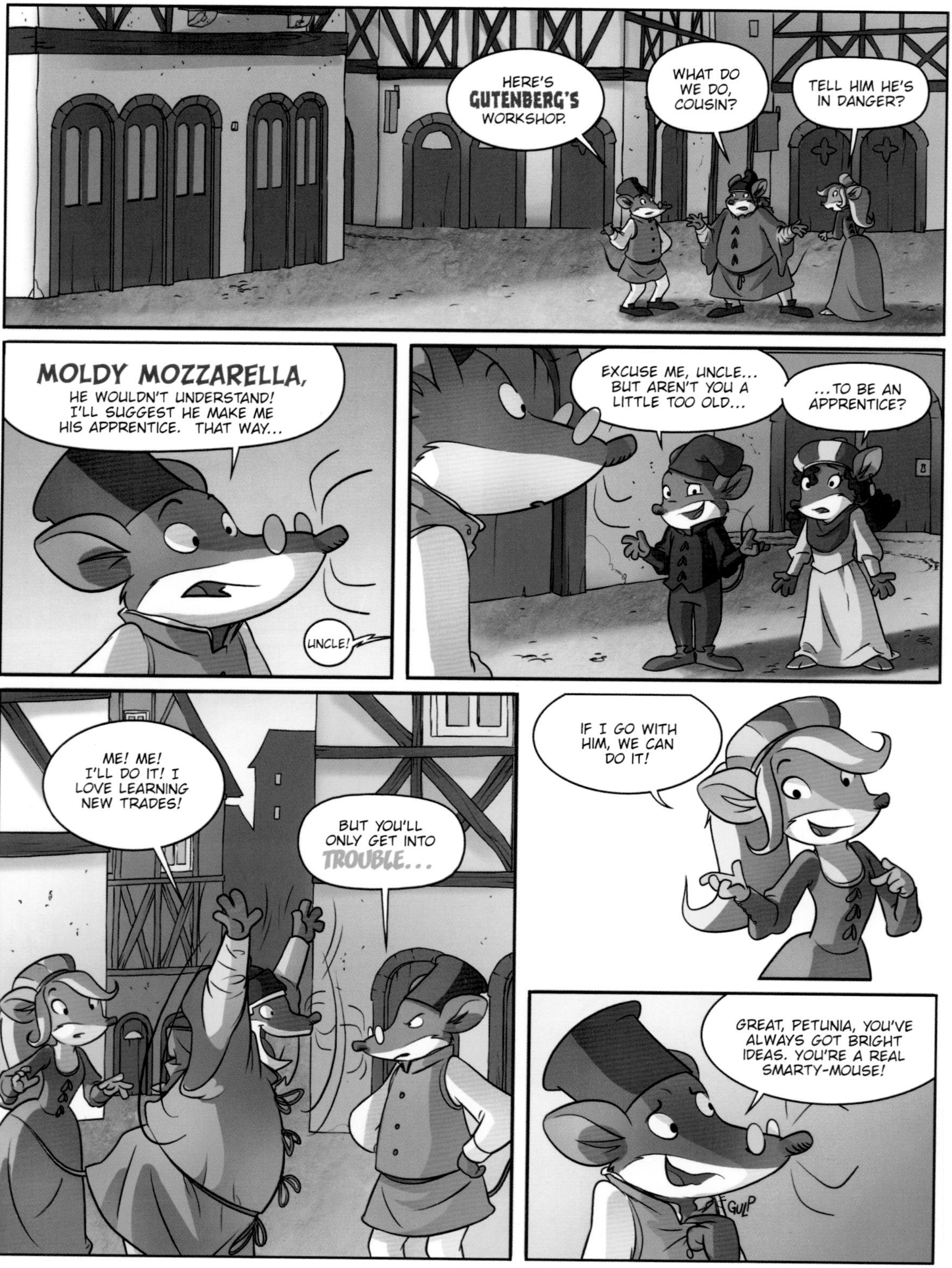
HERE'S GUTENBERG'S WORKSHOP.
WHAT DO WE DO, COUSIN?
TELL HIM HE'S IN DANGER?
MOLDY MOZZARELLA, HE WOULDN'T UNDERSTAND! I'LL SUGGEST HE MAKE ME HIS APPRENTICE. THAT WAY...
UNCLE!
EXCUSE ME, UNCLE... BUT AREN'T YOU A LITTLE TOO OLD...
...TO BE AN APPRENTICE?
ME! ME! I'LL DO IT! I LOVE LEARNING NEW TRADES!
BUT YOU'LL ONLY GET INTO TROUBLE...
IF I GO WITH HIM, WE CAN DO IT!
GREAT, PETUNIA, YOU'VE ALWAYS GOT BRIGHT IDEAS. YOU'RE A REAL SMARTY-MOUSE!
GULP

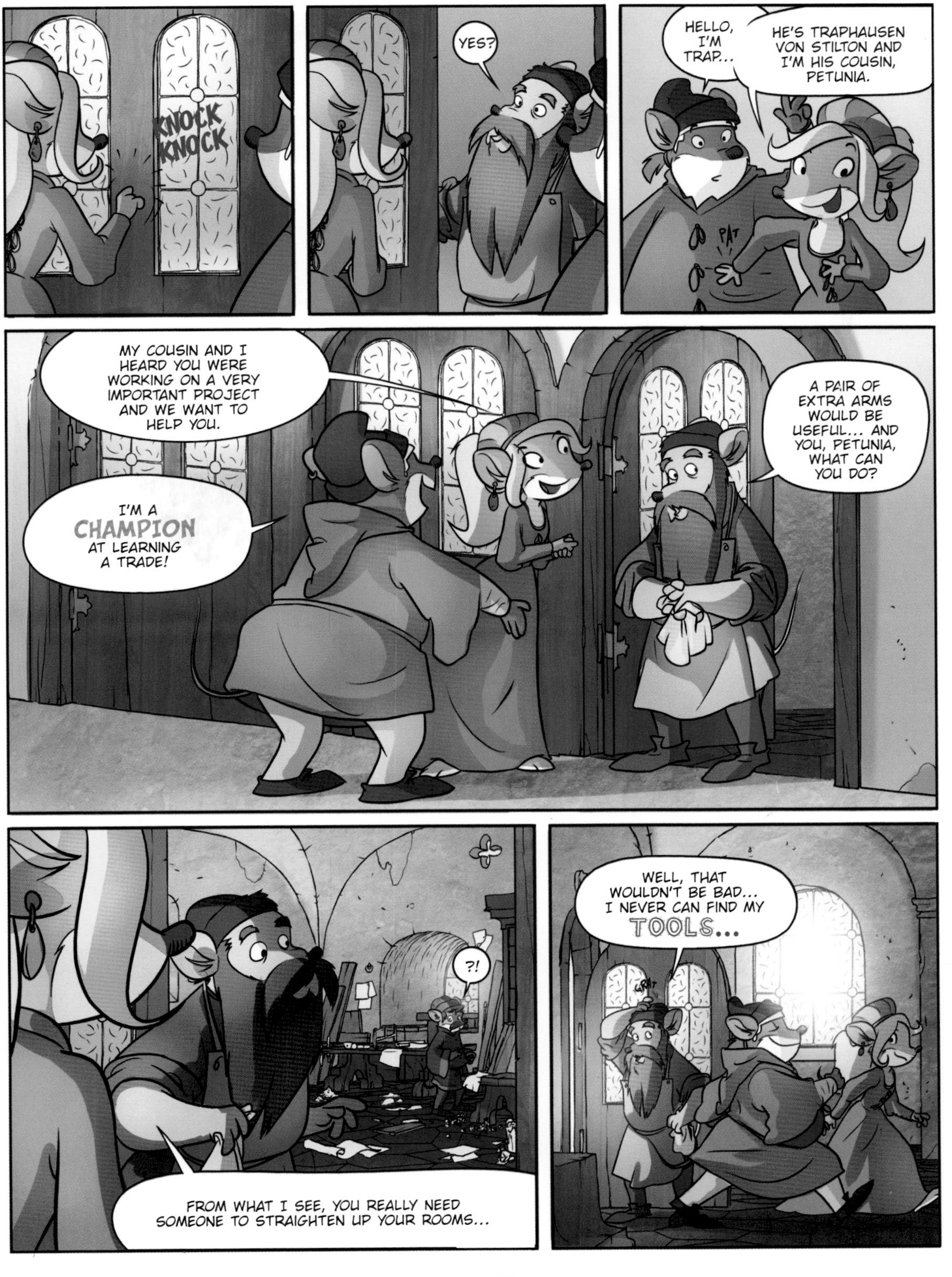
KNOCK KNOCK
YES?
HELLO, I'M TRAP...
HE'S TRAPHAUSEN VON STILTON AND I'M HIS COUSIN, PETUNIA.
PAT
MY COUSIN AND I HEARD YOU WERE WORKING ON A VERY IMPORTANT PROJECT AND WE WANT TO HELP YOU.
A PAIR OF EXTRA ARMS WOULD BE USEFUL... AND YOU, PETUNIA, WHAT CAN YOU DO?
I'M A CHAMPION AT LEARNING A TRADE!
?!
FROM WHAT I SEE, YOU REALLY NEED SOMEONE TO STRAIGHTEN UP YOUR ROOMS...
WELL, THAT WOULDN'T BE BAD... I NEVER CAN FIND MY TOOLS...

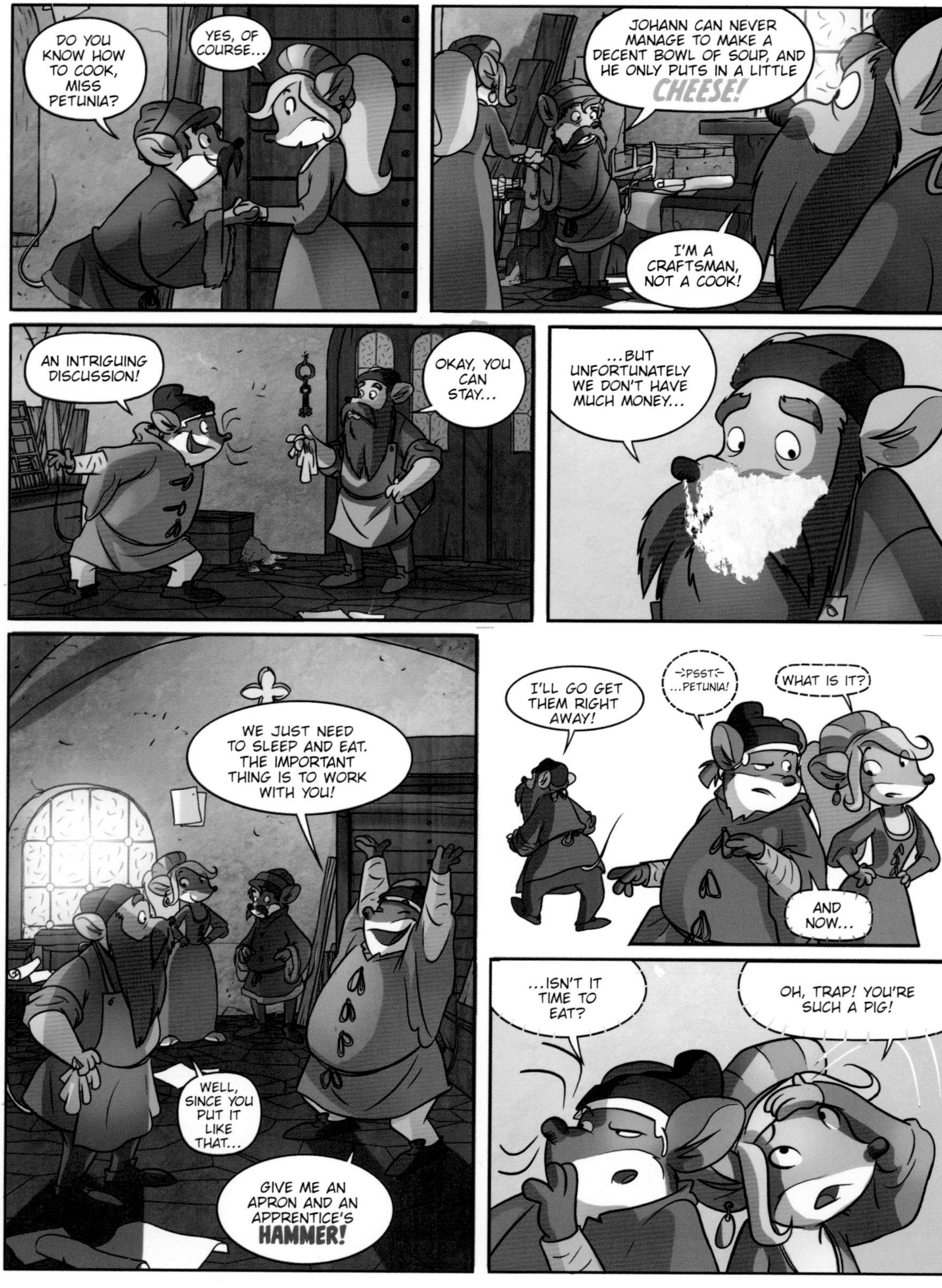
DO YOU KNOW HOW TO COOK, MISS PETUNIA?
YES, OF COURSE...
JOHANN CAN NEVER MANAGE TO MAKE A DECENT BOWL OF SOUP, AND HE ONLY PUTS IN A LITTLE CHEESE!
I'M A CRAFTSMAN, NOT A COOK!
AN INTRIGUING DISCUSSION!
OKAY, YOU CAN STAY...
...BUT UNFORTUNATELY WE DON'T HAVE MUCH MONEY...
WE JUST NEED TO SLEEP AND EAT. THE IMPORTANT THING IS TO WORK WITH YOU!
WELL, SINCE YOU PUT IT LIKE THAT...
GIVE ME AN APRON AND AN APPRENTICE'S HAMMER!
I'LL GO GET THEM RIGHT AWAY!
PSST... PETUNIA!
WHAT IS IT?
AND NOW...
...ISN'T IT TIME TO EAT?
OH, TRAP! YOU'RE SUCH A PIG!

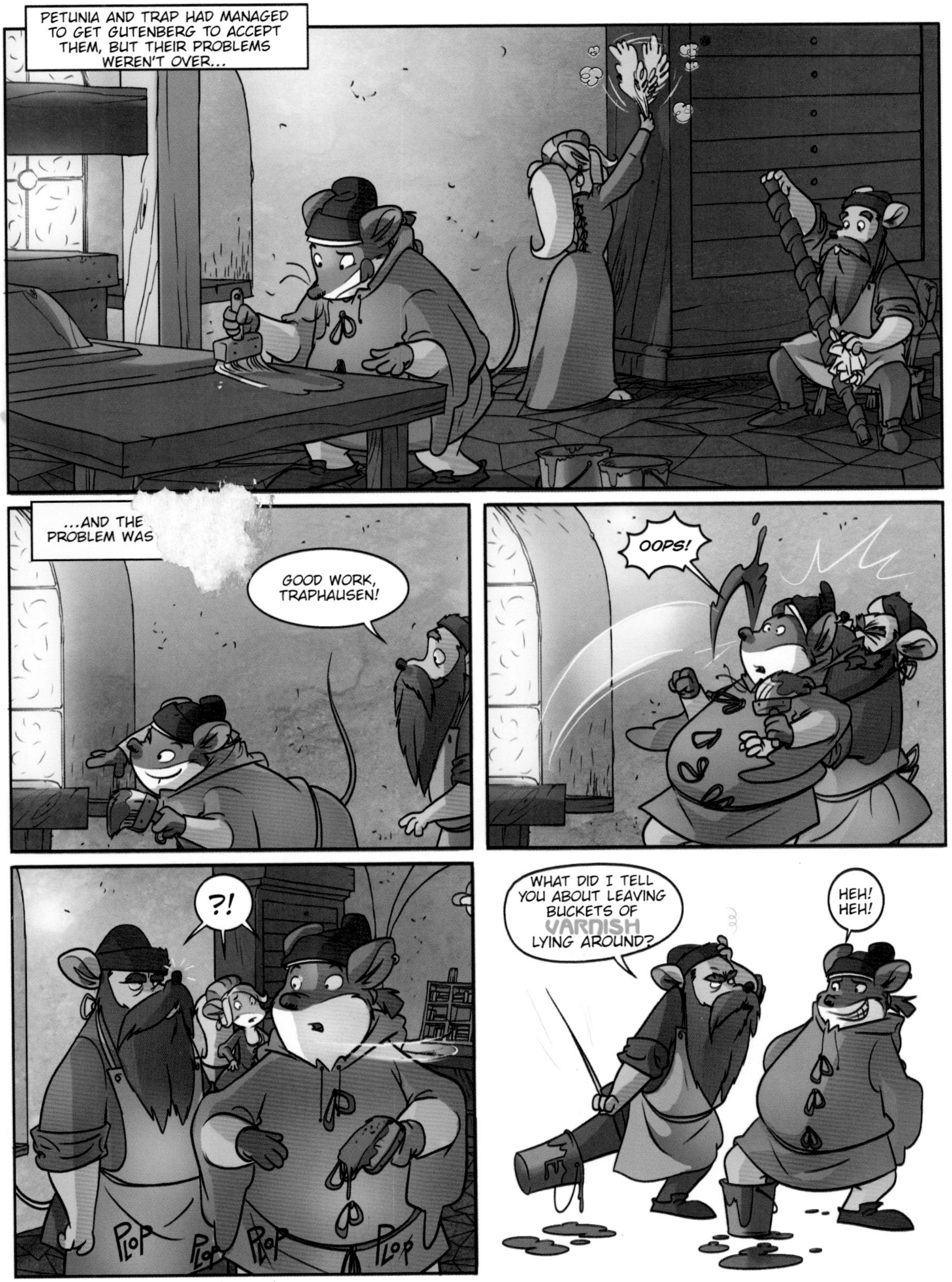

PETUNIA AND TRAP HAD MANAGED TO GET GUTENBERG TO ACCEPT THEM, BUT THEIR PROBLEMS WEREN'T OVER...
...AND THE
PROBLEM WAS
GOOD WORK, TRAPHAUSEN!
OOPS!
?!
PLOP
PLOP
PLOP
PLOP
WHAT DID I TELL YOU ABOUT LEAVING BUCKETS OF VARNISH LYING AROUND?
HEH! HEH!

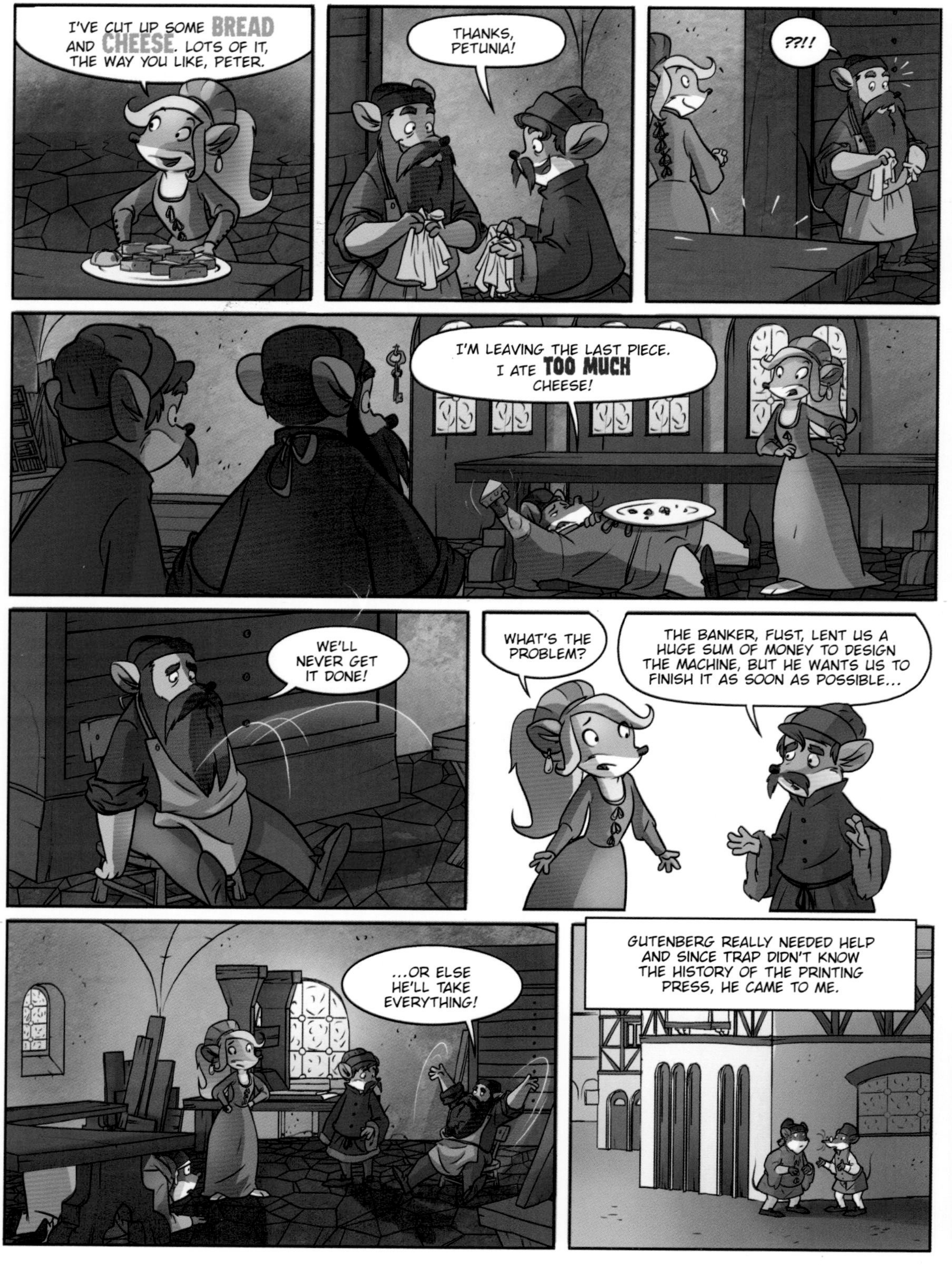

I'VE CUT UP SOME BREAD AND CHEESE. LOTS OF IT, THE WAY YOU LIKE, PETER.
THANKS, PETUNIA!
??!!
I'M LEAVING THE LAST PIECE. I ATE TOO MUCH CHEESE!
WE'LL NEVER GET IT DONE!
WHAT'S THE PROBLEM?
THE BANKER, FUST, LENT US A HUGE SUM OF MONEY TO DESIGN THE MACHINE, BUT HE WANTS US TO FINISH IT AS SOON AS POSSIBLE...
...OR ELSE HE'LL TAKE EVERYTHING!
GUTENBERG REALLY NEEDED HELP AND SINCE TRAP DIDN'T KNOW THE HISTORY OF THE PRINTING PRESS, HE CAME TO ME.

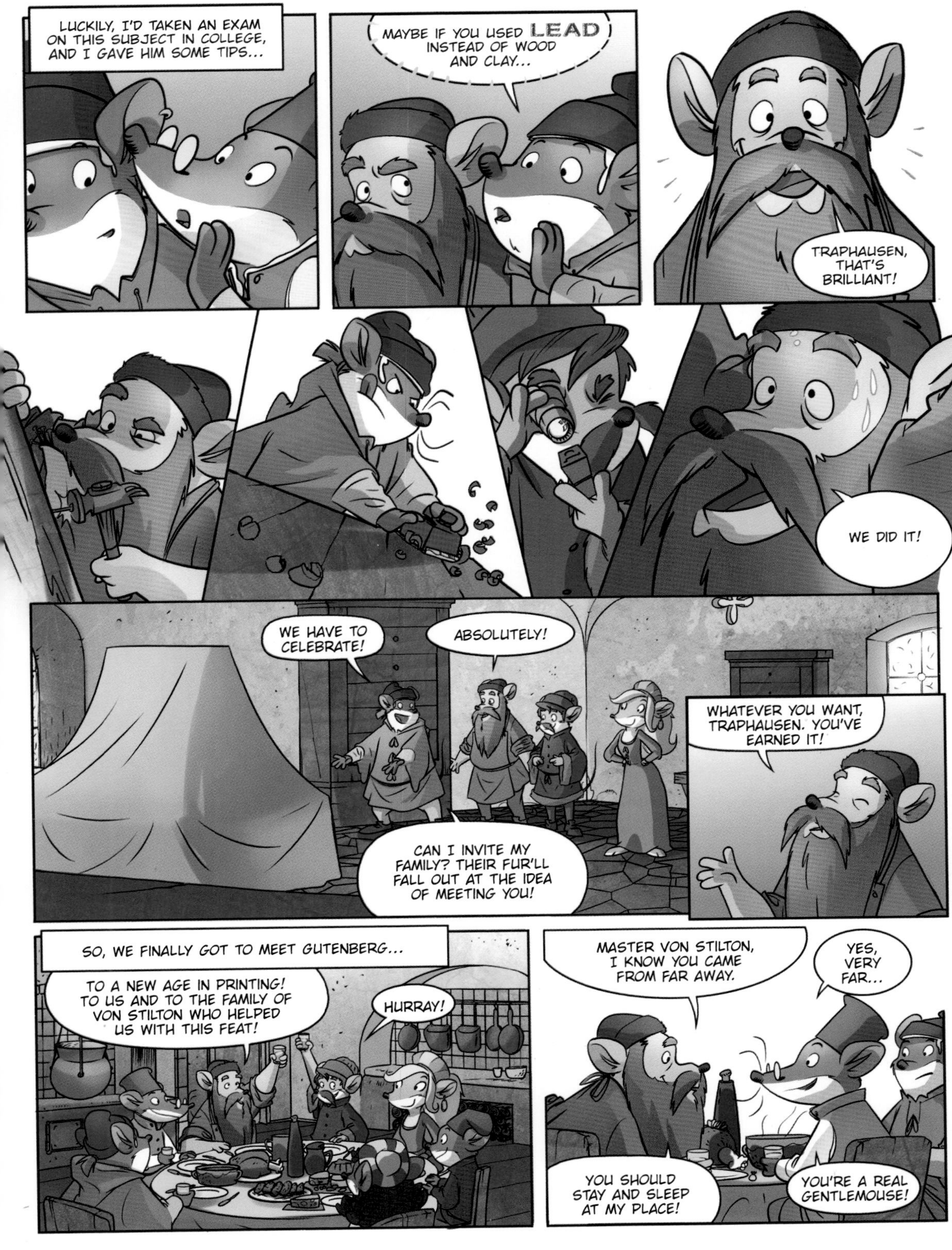

LUCKILY, I'D TAKEN AN EXAM ON THIS SUBJECT IN COLLEGE, AND I GAVE HIM SOME TIPS...
MAYBE IF YOU USED LEAD INSTEAD OF WOOD AND CLAY...
TRAPHAUSEN, THAT'S BRILLIANT!
WE DID IT!
WE HAVE TO CELEBRATE!
ABSOLUTELY!
CAN I INVITE MY FAMILY? THEIR FUR'LL FALL OUT AT THE IDEA OF MEETING YOU!
WHATEVER YOU WANT, TRAPHAUSEN. YOU'VE EARNED IT!
SO, WE FINALLY GOT TO MEET GUTENBERG...
TO A NEW AGE IN PRINTING! TO US AND TO THE FAMILY OF VON STILTON WHO HELPED US WITH THIS FEAT!
HURRAY!
MASTER VON STILTON, I KNOW YOU CAME FROM FAR AWAY.
YES, VERY FAR...
YOU SHOULD STAY AND SLEEP AT MY PLACE!
YOU'RE A REAL GENTLEMOUSE!

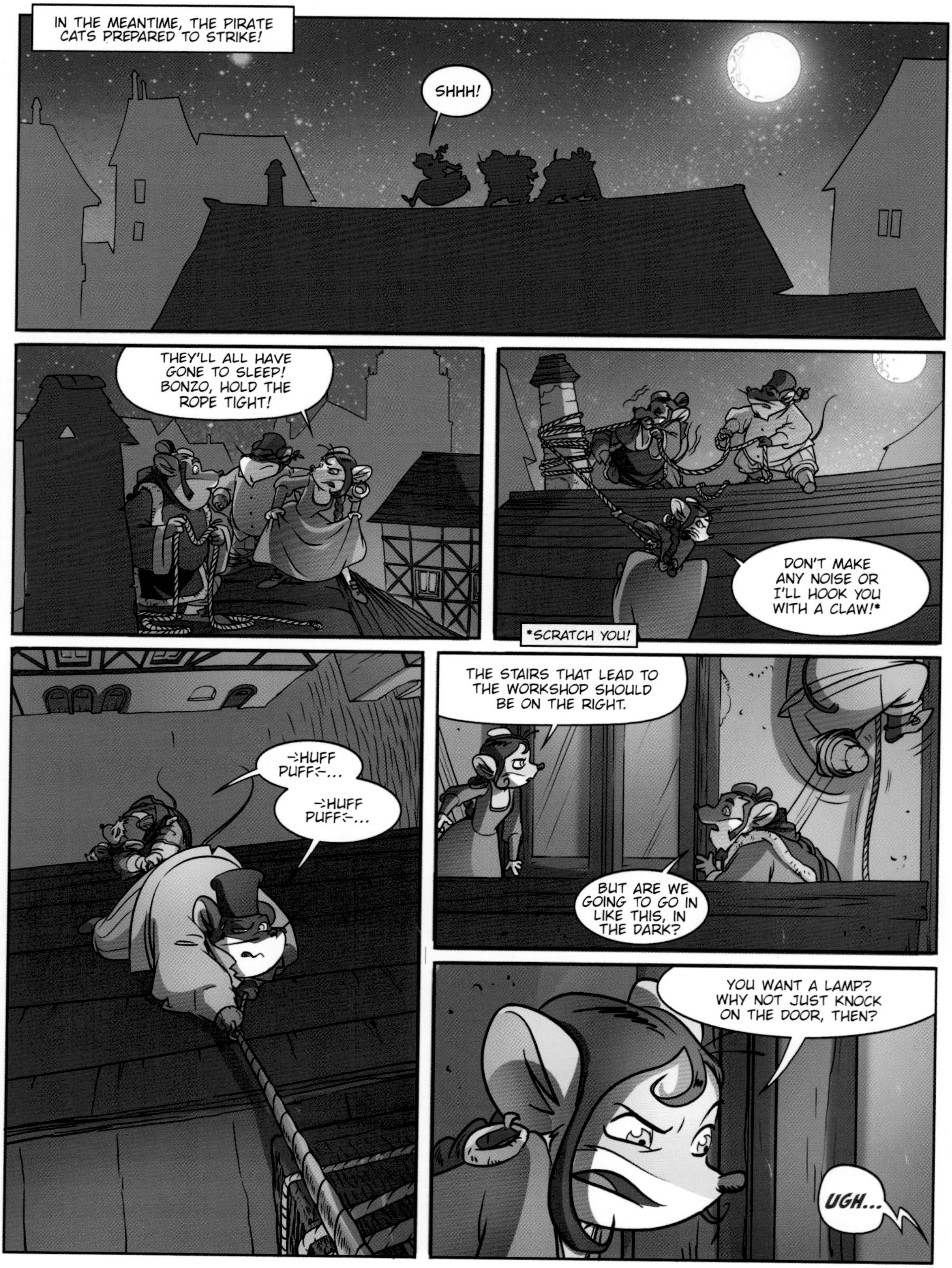
IN THE MEANTIME, THE PIRATE CATS PREPARED TO STRIKE!
SHHH!
THEY'LL ALL HAVE GONE TO SLEEP! BONZO, HOLD THE ROPE TIGHT!
DON'T MAKE ANY NOISE OR I'LL HOOK YOU WITH A CLAW!*
*SCRATCH YOU!
→HUFF PUFF←...
→HUFF PUFF←...
THE STAIRS THAT LEAD TO THE WORKSHOP SHOULD BE ON THE RIGHT.
BUT ARE WE GOING TO GO IN LIKE THIS, IN THE DARK?
YOU WANT A LAMP? WHY NOT JUST KNOCK ON THE DOOR, THEN?
UGH...

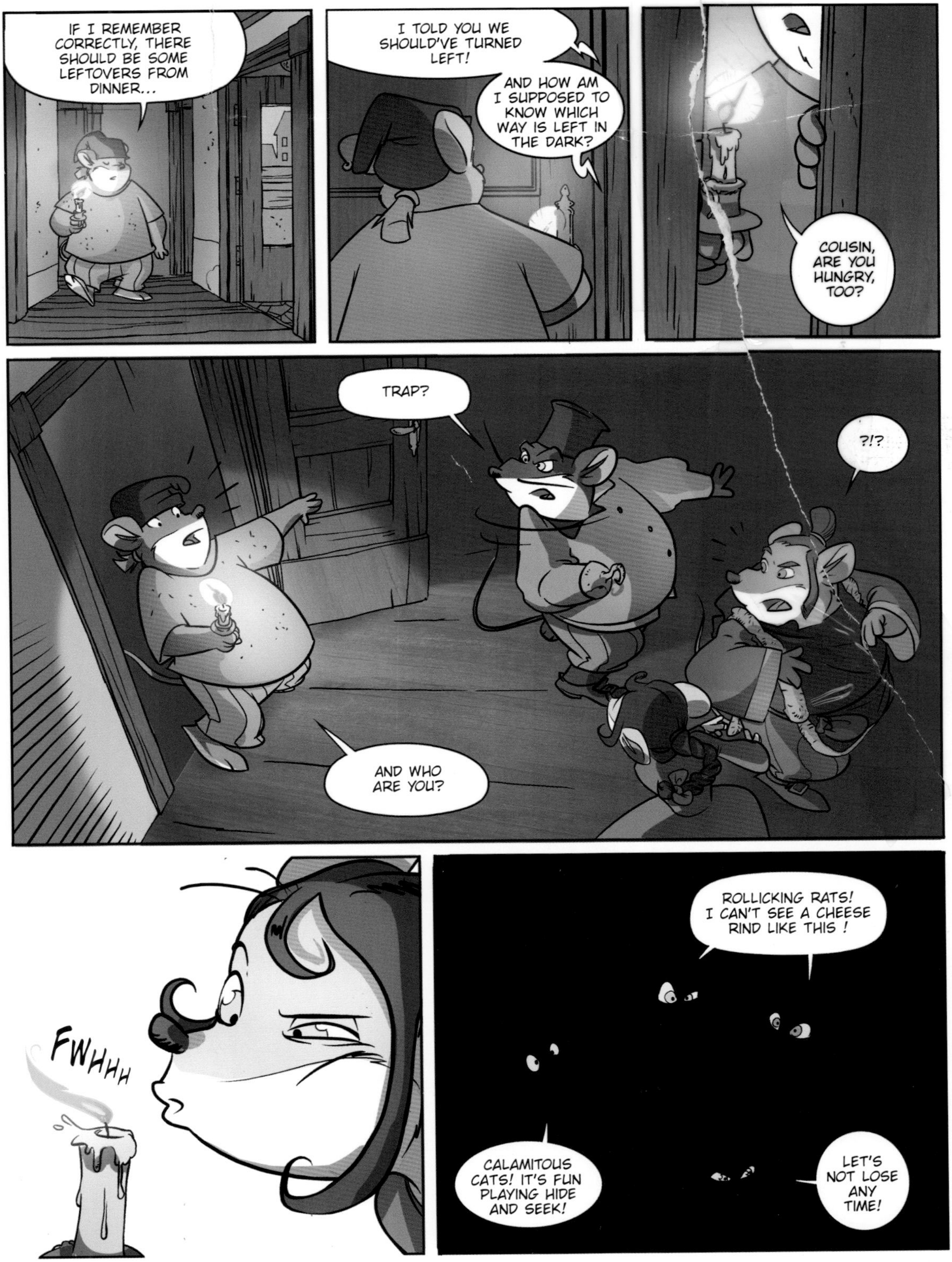
IF I REMEMBER CORRECTLY, THERE SHOULD BE SOME LEFTOVERS FROM DINNER...
I TOLD YOU WE SHOULD'VE TURNED LEFT!
AND HOW AM I SUPPOSED TO KNOW WHICH WAY IS LEFT IN THE DARK?
COUSIN, ARE YOU HUNGRY, TOO?
TRAP?
?!?
AND WHO ARE YOU?
FWHHH
ROLLICKING RATS! I CAN'T SEE A CHEESE RIND LIKE THIS !
CALAMITOUS CATS! IT'S FUN PLAYING HIDE AND SEEK!
LET'S NOT LOSE ANY TIME!

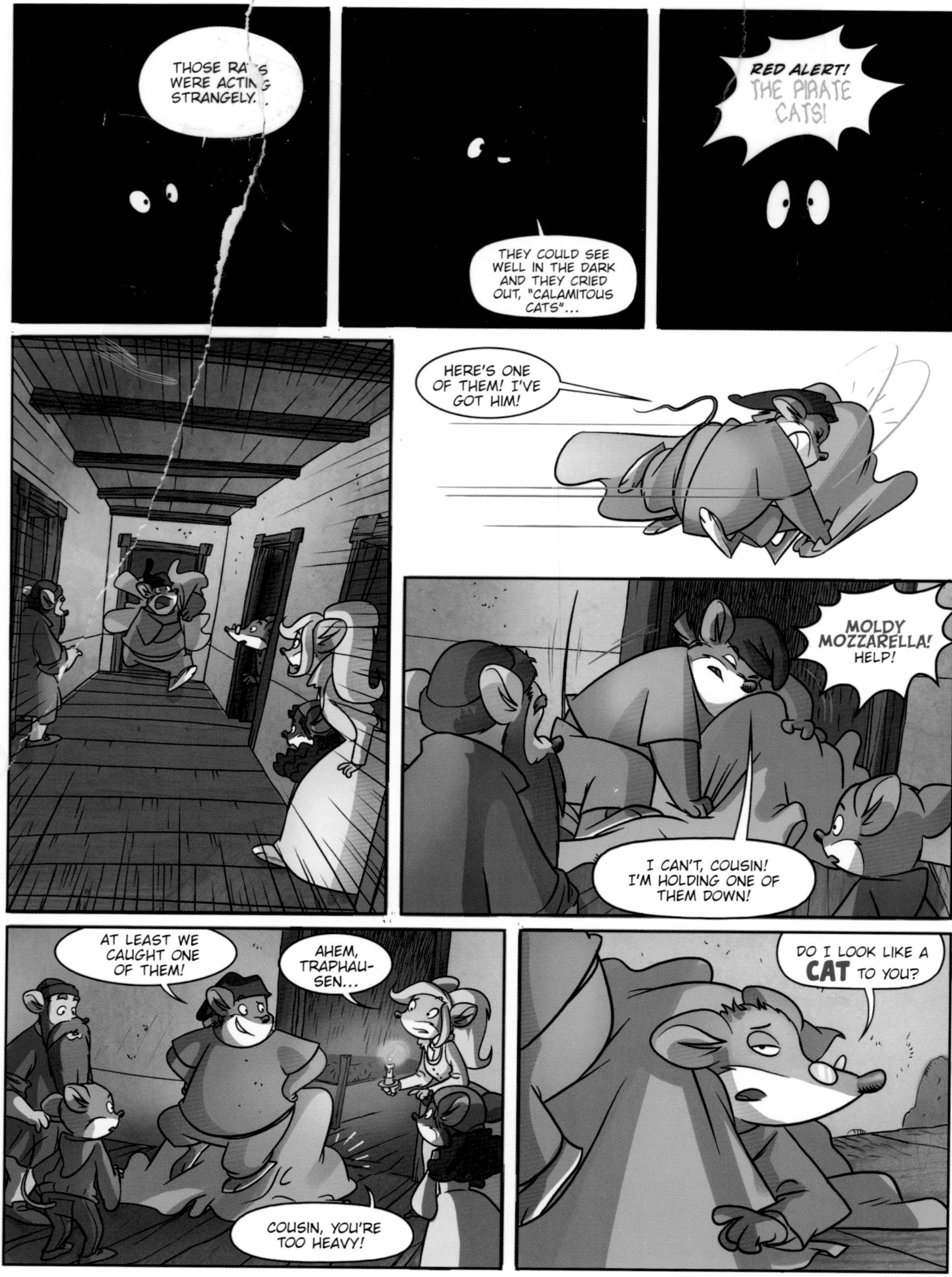
THOSE RATS WERE ACTING STRANGELY...
THEY COULD SEE WELL IN THE DARK AND THEY CRIED OUT, "CALAMITOUS CATS"...
RED ALERT! THE PIRATE CATS!
HERE'S ONE OF THEM! I'VE GOT HIM!
MOLDY MOZZARELLA! HELP!
I CAN'T, COUSIN! I'M HOLDING ONE OF THEM DOWN!
AT LEAST WE CAUGHT ONE OF THEM!
AHEM, TRAPHAU-SEN...
COUSIN, YOU'RE TOO HEAVY!
DO I LOOK LIKE A CAT TO YOU?

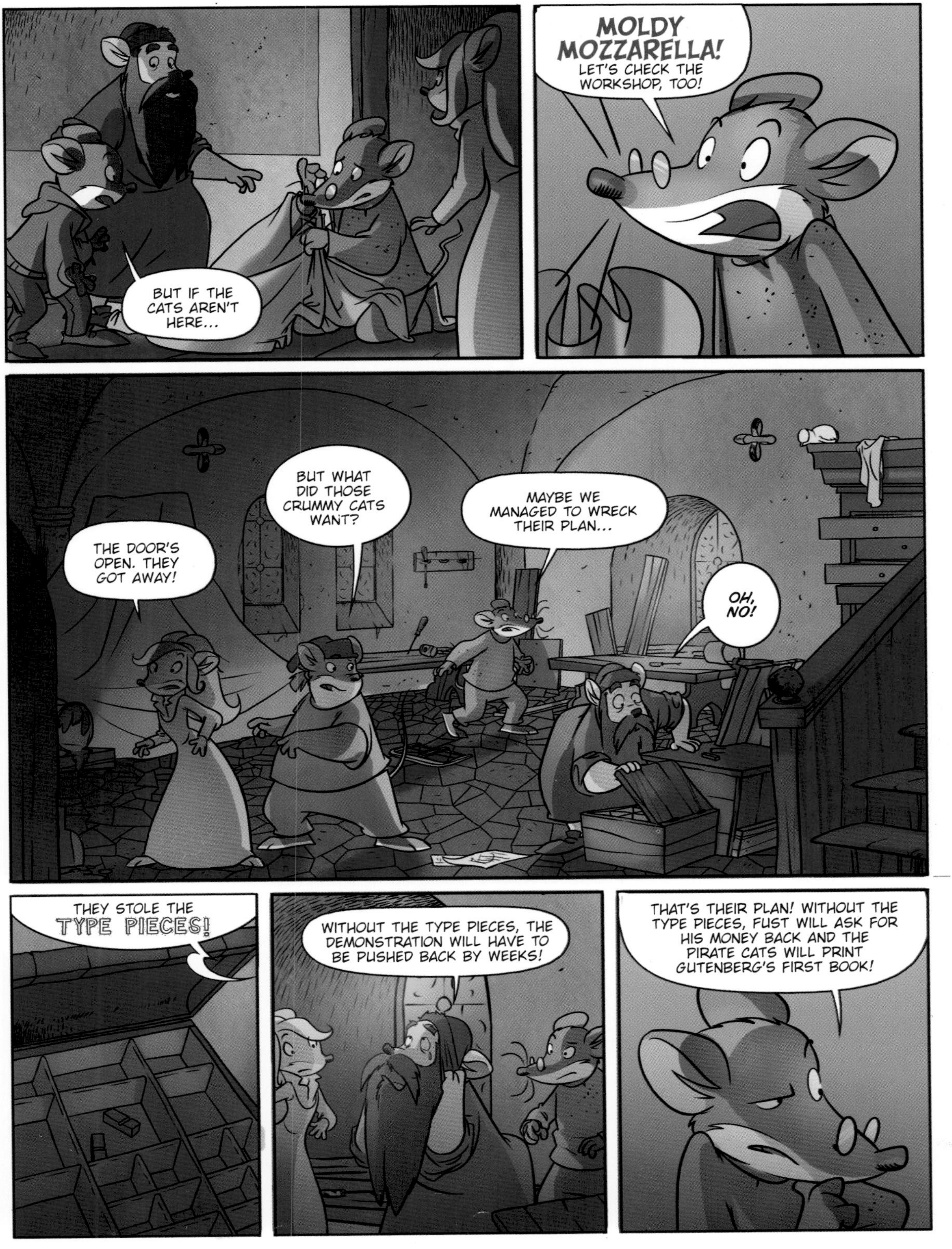
BUT IF THE CATS AREN'T HERE...
MOLDY MOZZARELLA! LET'S CHECK THE WORKSHOP, TOO!
THE DOOR'S OPEN. THEY GOT AWAY!
BUT WHAT DID THOSE CRUMMY CATS WANT?
MAYBE WE MANAGED TO WRECK THEIR PLAN...
OH, NO!
THEY STOLE THE TYPE PIECES!
WITHOUT THE TYPE PIECES, THE DEMONSTRATION WILL HAVE TO BE PUSHED BACK BY WEEKS!
THAT'S THEIR PLAN! WITHOUT THE TYPE PIECES, FUST WILL ASK FOR HIS MONEY BACK AND THE PIRATE CATS WILL PRINT GUTENBERG'S FIRST BOOK!

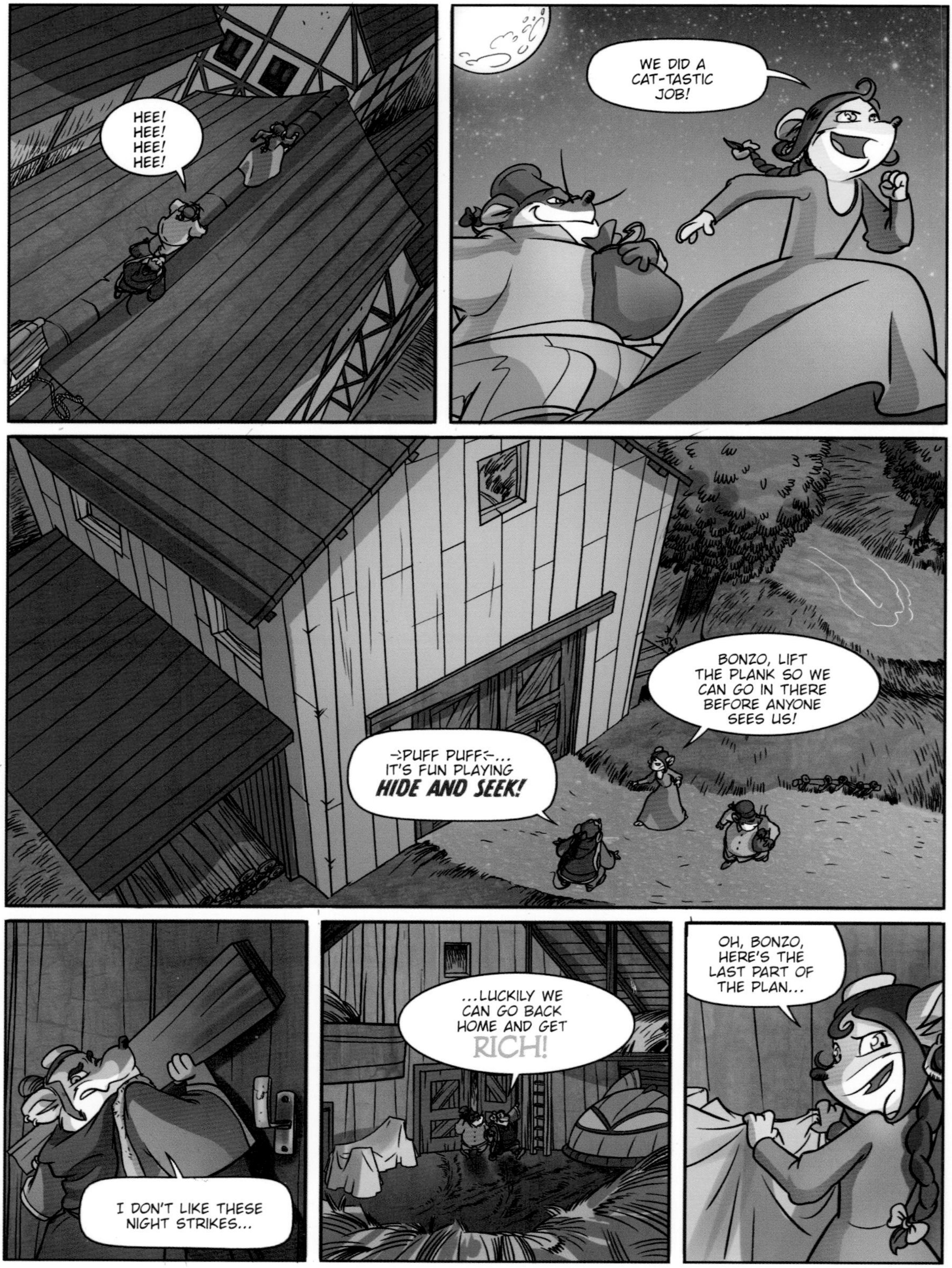
HEE!
HEE!
HEE!
HEE!
WE DID A CAT-TASTIC JOB!
BONZO, LIFT THE PLANK SO WE CAN GO IN THERE BEFORE ANYONE SEES US!
PUFF PUFF... IT'S FUN PLAYING HIDE AND SEEK!
I DON'T LIKE THESE NIGHT STRIKES...
...LUCKILY WE CAN GO BACK HOME AND GET RICH!
OH, BONZO, HERE'S THE LAST PART OF THE PLAN...

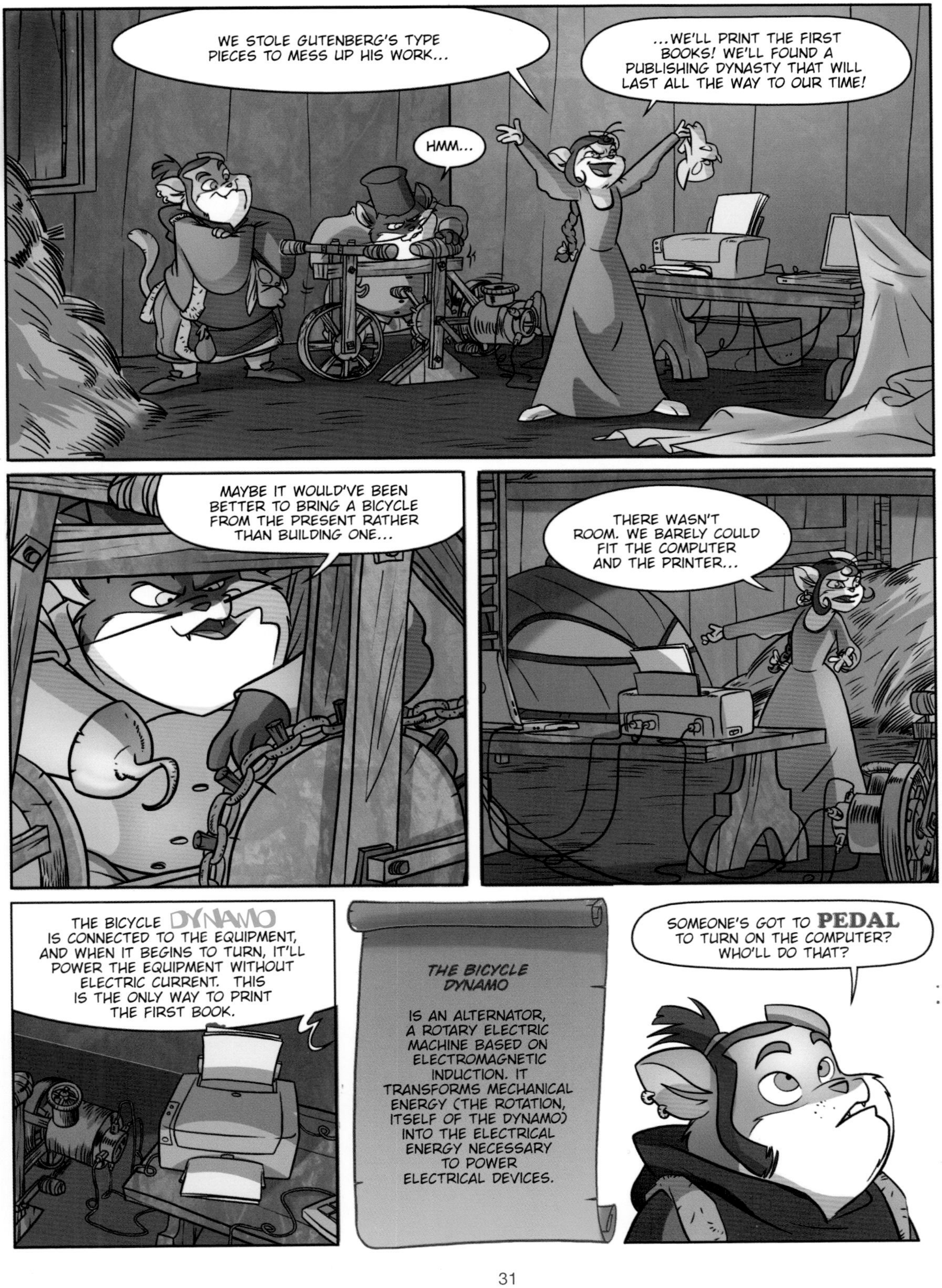
WE STOLE GUTENBERG'S TYPE PIECES TO MESS UP HIS WORK...
...WE'LL PRINT THE FIRST BOOKS! WE'LL FOUND A PUBLISHING DYNASTY THAT WILL LAST ALL THE WAY TO OUR TIME!
HMM...
MAYBE IT WOULD'VE BEEN BETTER TO BRING A BICYCLE FROM THE PRESENT RATHER THAN BUILDING ONE...
THERE WASN'T ROOM. WE BARELY COULD FIT THE COMPUTER AND THE PRINTER...
THE BICYCLE DYNAMO IS CONNECTED TO THE EQUIPMENT, AND WHEN IT BEGINS TO TURN, IT'LL POWER THE EQUIPMENT WITHOUT ELECTRIC CURRENT. THIS IS THE ONLY WAY TO PRINT THE FIRST BOOK.
THE BICYCLE DYNAMO
IS AN ALTERNATOR, A ROTARY ELECTRIC MACHINE BASED ON ELECTROMAGNETIC INDUCTION. IT TRANSFORMS MECHANICAL ENERGY (THE ROTATION, ITSELF OF THE DYNAMO) INTO THE ELECTRICAL ENERGY NECESSARY TO POWER ELECTRICAL DEVICES.
SOMEONE'S GOT TO PEDAL TO TURN ON THE COMPUTER? WHO'LL DO THAT?

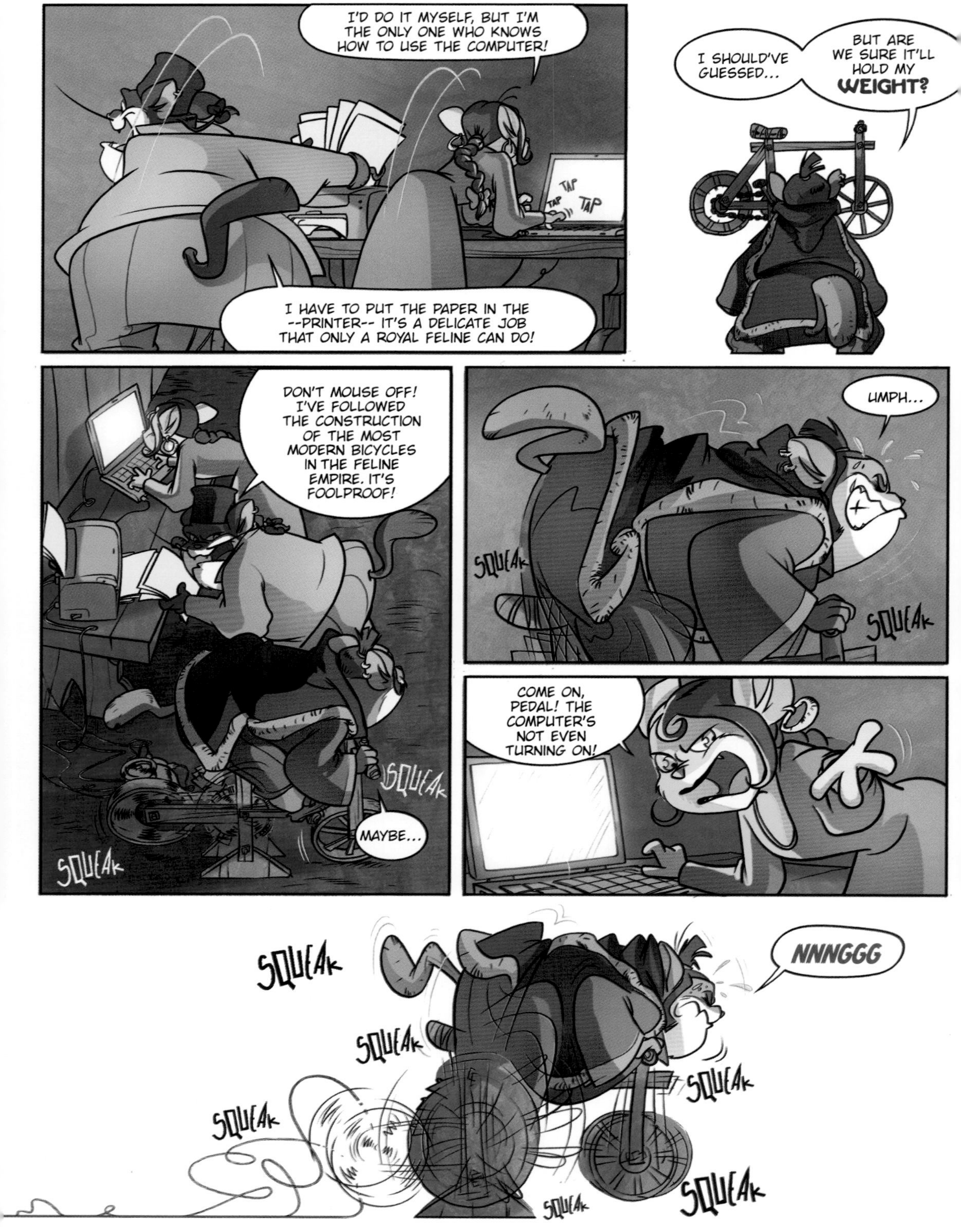

I'D DO IT MYSELF, BUT I'M THE ONLY ONE WHO KNOWS HOW TO USE THE COMPUTER!
TAP TAP TAP
I HAVE TO PUT THE PAPER IN THE --PRINTER-- IT'S A DELICATE JOB THAT ONLY A ROYAL FELINE CAN DO!
I SHOULD'VE GUESSED...
BUT ARE WE SURE IT'LL HOLD MY WEIGHT?
DON'T MOUSE OFF! I'VE FOLLOWED THE CONSTRUCTION OF THE MOST MODERN BICYCLES IN THE FELINE EMPIRE. IT'S FOOLPROOF!
SQUEAK
MAYBE...
SQUEAK
UMPH...
SQUEAK
SQUEAK
COME ON, PEDAL! THE COMPUTER'S NOT EVEN TURNING ON!
SQUEAK
NNNGGG
SQUEAK
SQUEAK
SQUEAK
SQUEAK
SQUEAK
SQUEAK

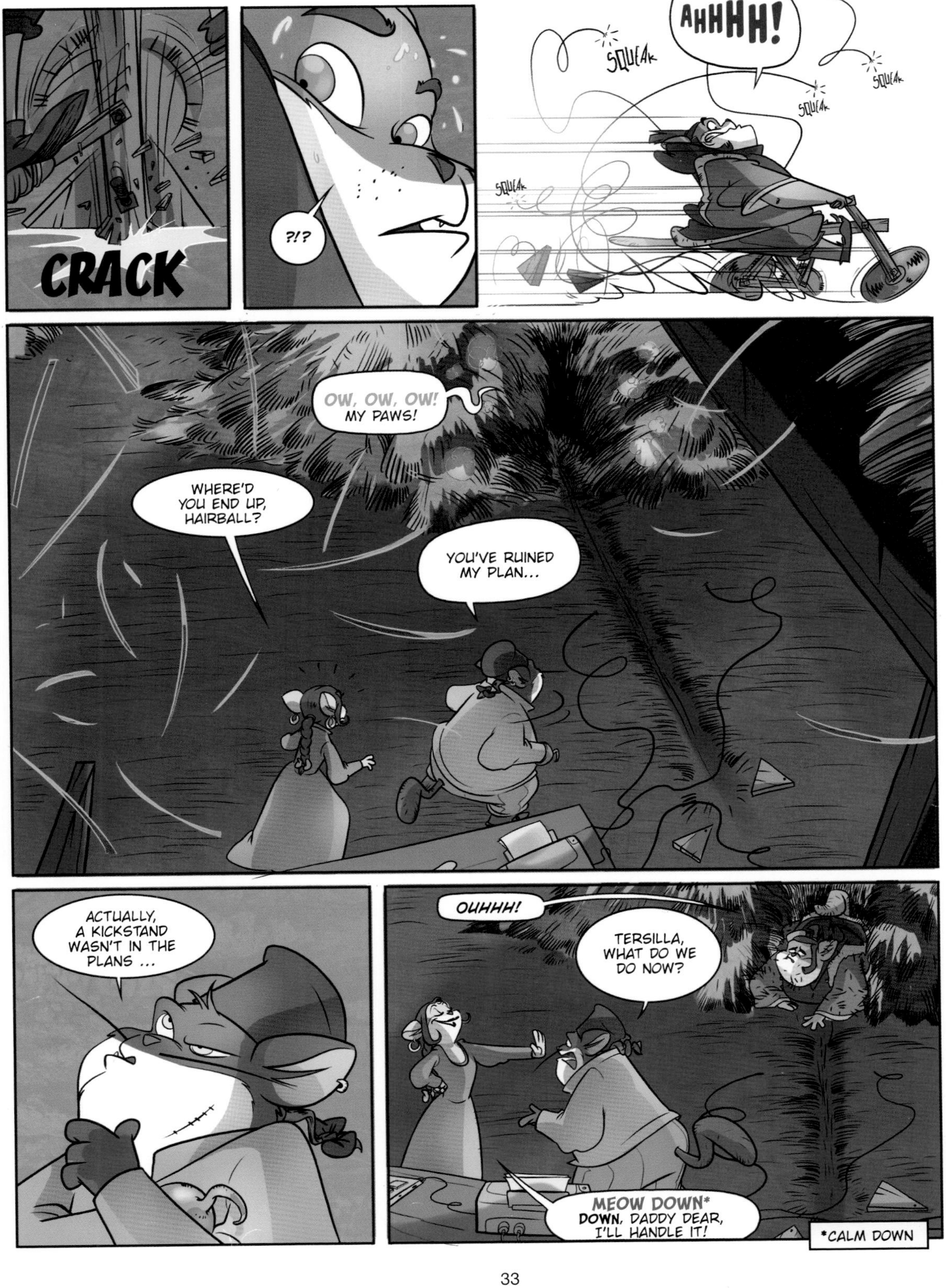
CRACK
?!?
AHHHH!
SQUEAK
SQUEAK
SQUEAK
SQUEAK
OW, OW, OW! MY PAWS!
WHERE'D YOU END UP, HAIRBALL?
YOU'VE RUINED MY PLAN...
ACTUALLY, A KICKSTAND WASN'T IN THE PLANS ...
OUHHH!
TERSILLA, WHAT DO WE DO NOW?
MEOW DOWN* DOWN, DADDY DEAR, I'LL HANDLE IT!
*CALM DOWN

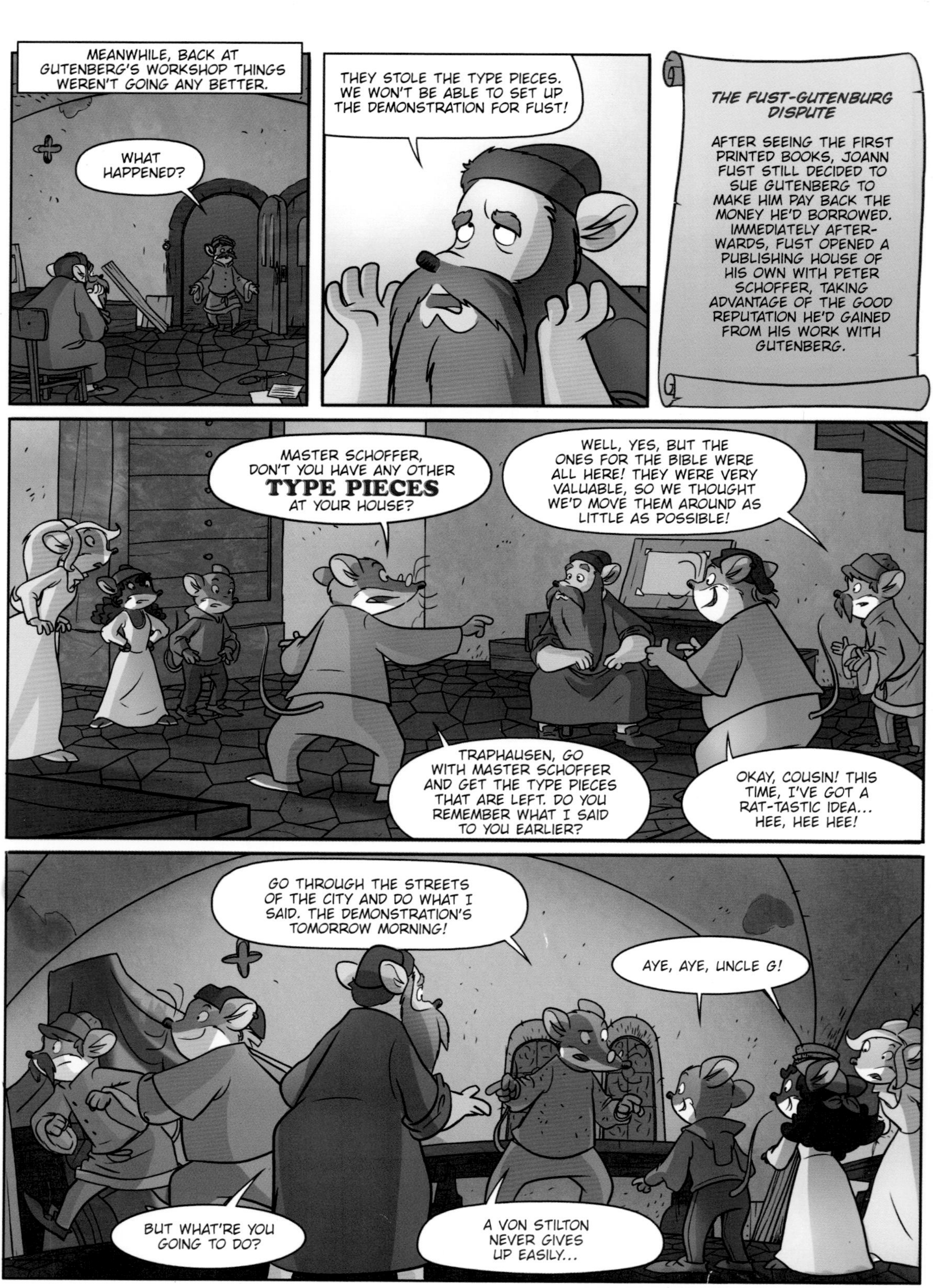
MEANWHILE, BACK AT GUTENBERG'S WORKSHOP THINGS WEREN'T GOING ANY BETTER.
WHAT HAPPENED?
THEY STOLE THE TYPE PIECES. WE WON'T BE ABLE TO SET UP THE DEMONSTRATION FOR FUST!
THE FUST-GUTENBURG DISPUTE
AFTER SEEING THE FIRST PRINTED BOOKS, JOANN FUST STILL DECIDED TO SUE GUTENBERG TO MAKE HIM PAY BACK THE MONEY HE'D BORROWED. IMMEDIATELY AFTER-WARDS, FUST OPENED A PUBLISHING HOUSE OF HIS OWN WITH PETER SCHOFFER, TAKING ADVANTAGE OF THE GOOD REPUTATION HE'D GAINED FROM HIS WORK WITH GUTENBERG.
MASTER SCHOFFER, DON'T YOU HAVE ANY OTHER TYPE PIECES AT YOUR HOUSE?
WELL, YES, BUT THE ONES FOR THE BIBLE WERE ALL HERE! THEY WERE VERY VALUABLE, SO WE THOUGHT WE'D MOVE THEM AROUND AS LITTLE AS POSSIBLE!
TRAPHAUSEN, GO WITH MASTER SCHOFFER AND GET THE TYPE PIECES THAT ARE LEFT. DO YOU REMEMBER WHAT I SAID TO YOU EARLIER?
OKAY, COUSIN! THIS TIME, I'VE GOT A RAT-TASTIC IDEA... HEE, HEE HEE!
GO THROUGH THE STREETS OF THE CITY AND DO WHAT I SAID. THE DEMONSTRATION'S TOMORROW MORNING!
AYE, AYE, UNCLE G!
BUT WHAT'RE YOU GOING TO DO?
A VON STILTON NEVER GIVES UP EASILY...

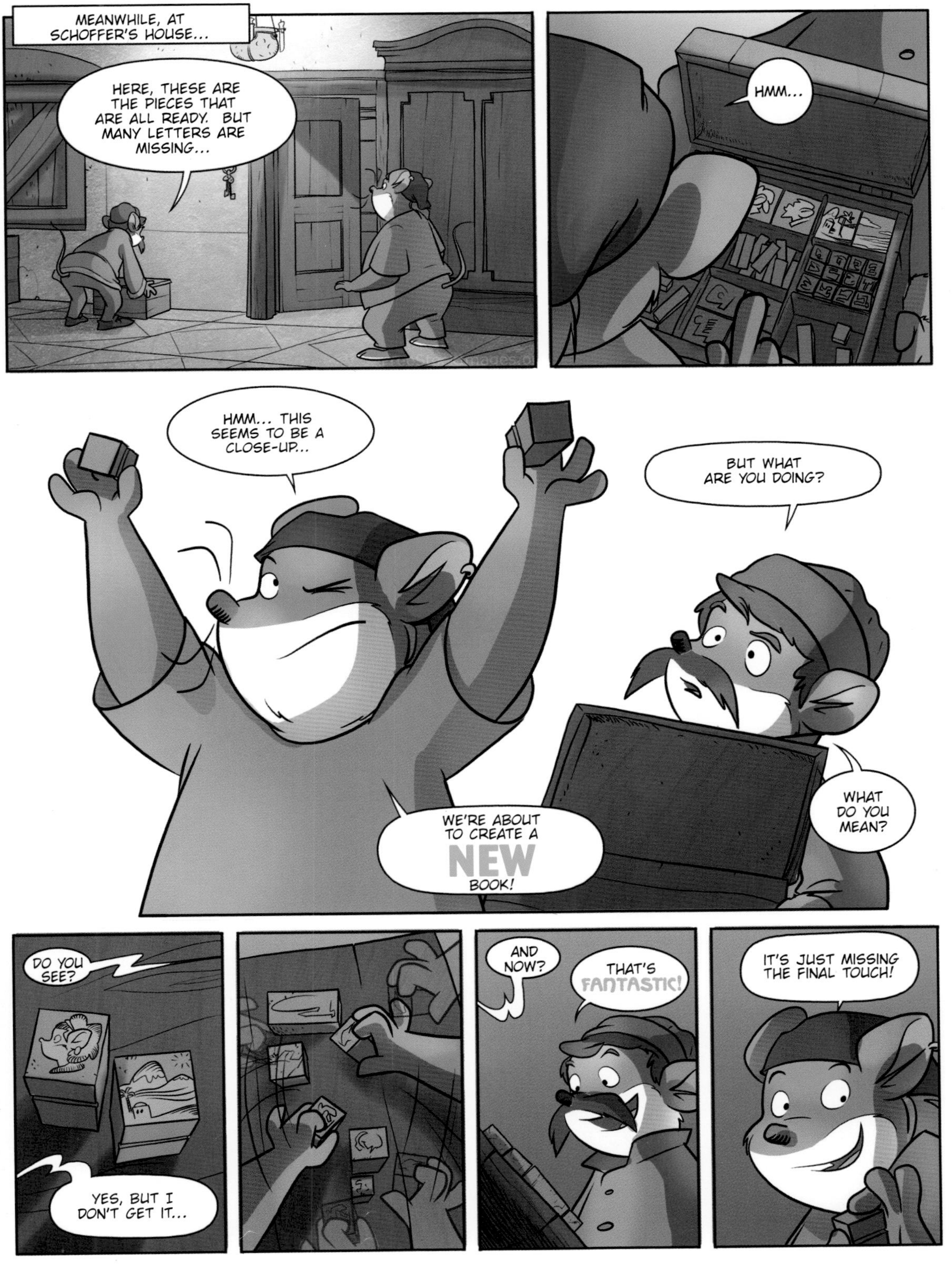
MEANWHILE, AT SCHOFFER'S HOUSE...
HERE, THESE ARE THE PIECES THAT ARE ALL READY. BUT MANY LETTERS ARE MISSING...
HMM...
HMM... THIS SEEMS TO BE A CLOSE-UP...
BUT WHAT ARE YOU DOING?
WE'RE ABOUT TO CREATE A NEW BOOK!
WHAT DO YOU MEAN?
DO YOU SEE?
YES, BUT I DON'T GET IT...
AND NOW?
THAT'S FANTASTIC!
IT'S JUST MISSING THE FINAL TOUCH!

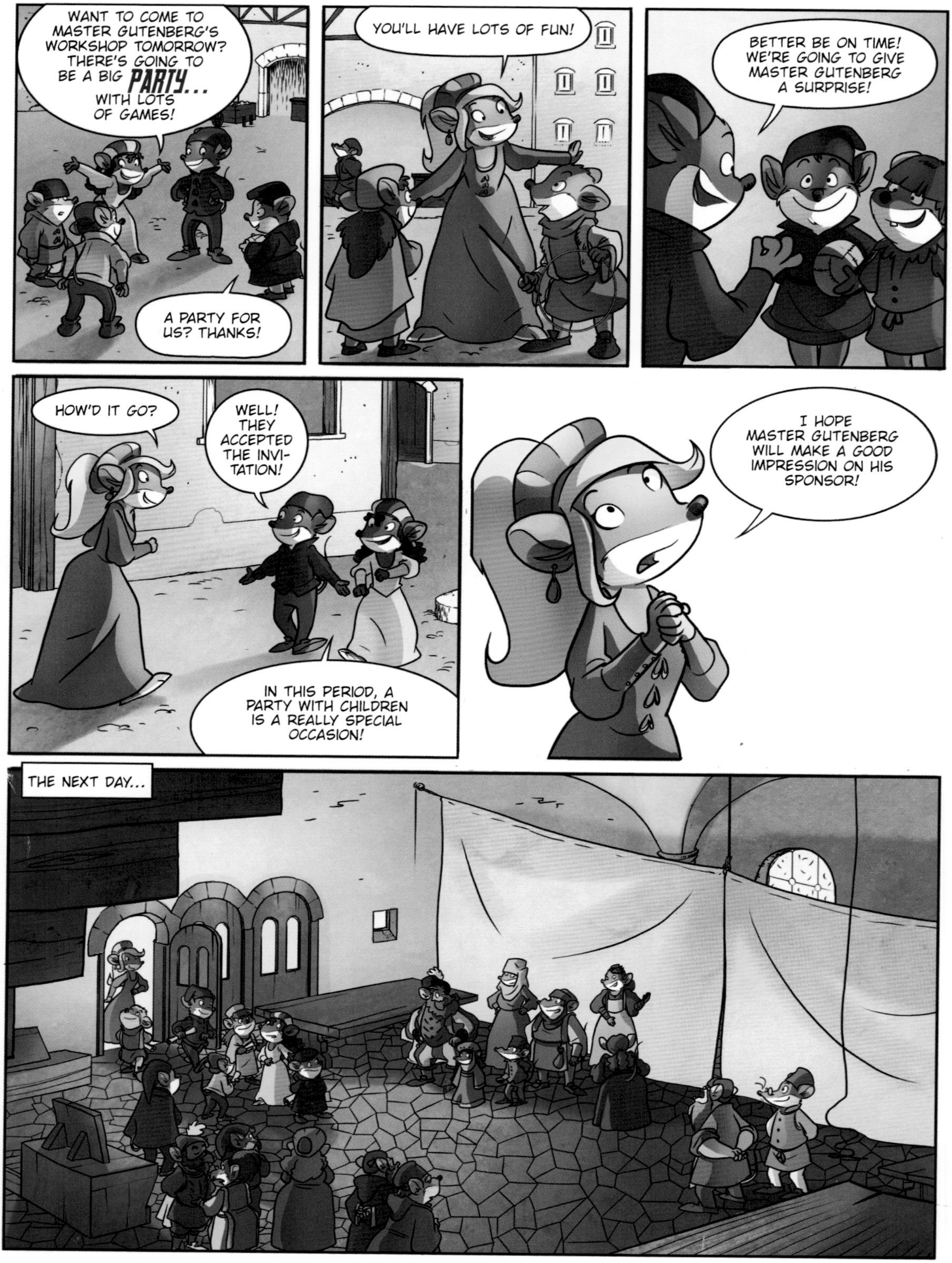
WANT TO COME TO MASTER GUTENBERG'S WORKSHOP TOMORROW? THERE'S GOING TO BE A BIG PARTY... WITH LOTS OF GAMES!
A PARTY FOR US? THANKS!
YOU'LL HAVE LOTS OF FUN!
BETTER BE ON TIME! WE'RE GOING TO GIVE MASTER GUTENBERG A SURPRISE!
HOW'D IT GO?
WELL! THEY ACCEPTED THE INVI-TATION!
IN THIS PERIOD, A PARTY WITH CHILDREN IS A REALLY SPECIAL OCCASION!
I HOPE MASTER GUTENBERG WILL MAKE A GOOD IMPRESSION ON HIS SPONSOR!
THE NEXT DAY...

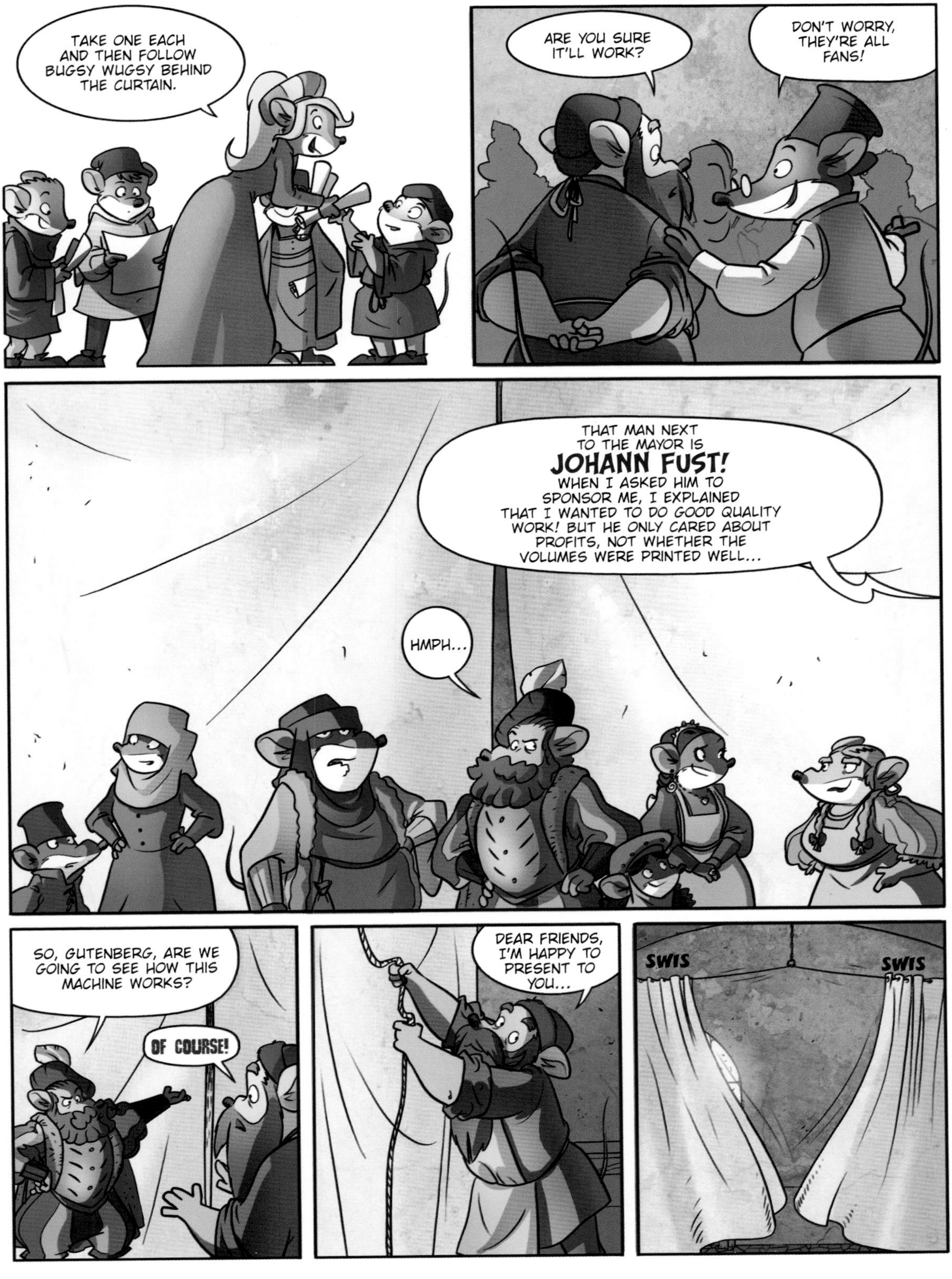
TAKE ONE EACH AND THEN FOLLOW BUGSY WUGSY BEHIND THE CURTAIN.
ARE YOU SURE IT'LL WORK?
DON'T WORRY, THEY'RE ALL FANS!
THAT MAN NEXT TO THE MAYOR IS JOHANN FUST! WHEN I ASKED HIM TO SPONSOR ME, I EXPLAINED THAT I WANTED TO DO GOOD QUALITY WORK! BUT HE ONLY CARED ABOUT PROFITS, NOT WHETHER THE VOLUMES WERE PRINTED WELL...
HMPH...
SO, GUTENBERG, ARE WE GOING TO SEE HOW THIS MACHINE WORKS?
OF COURSE!
DEAR FRIENDS, I'M HAPPY TO PRESENT TO YOU...
SWIS
SWIS

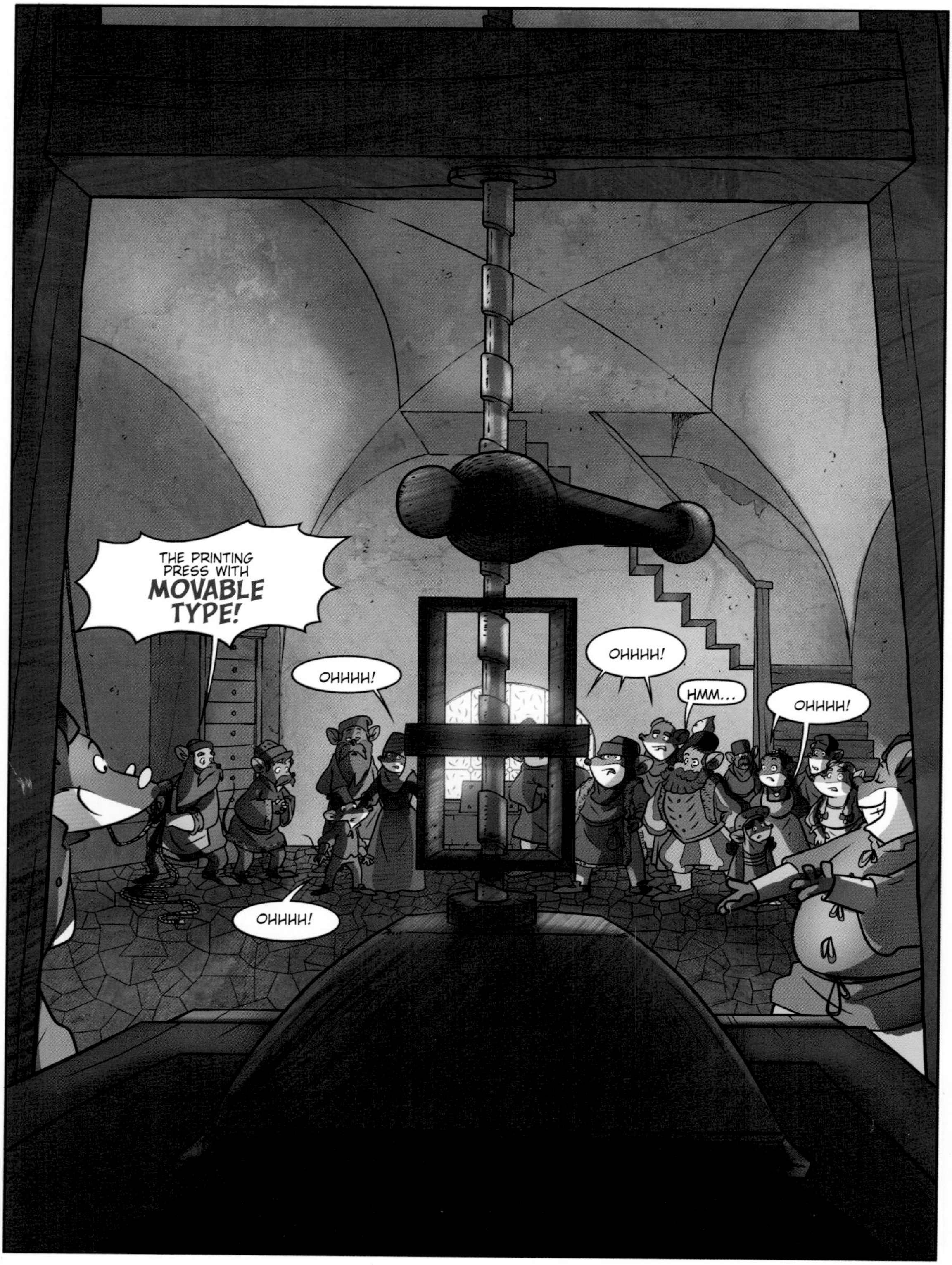
THE PRINTING PRESS WITH MOVABLE TYPE!
OHHHH!
OHHHH!
HMM...
OHHHH!
OHHHH!

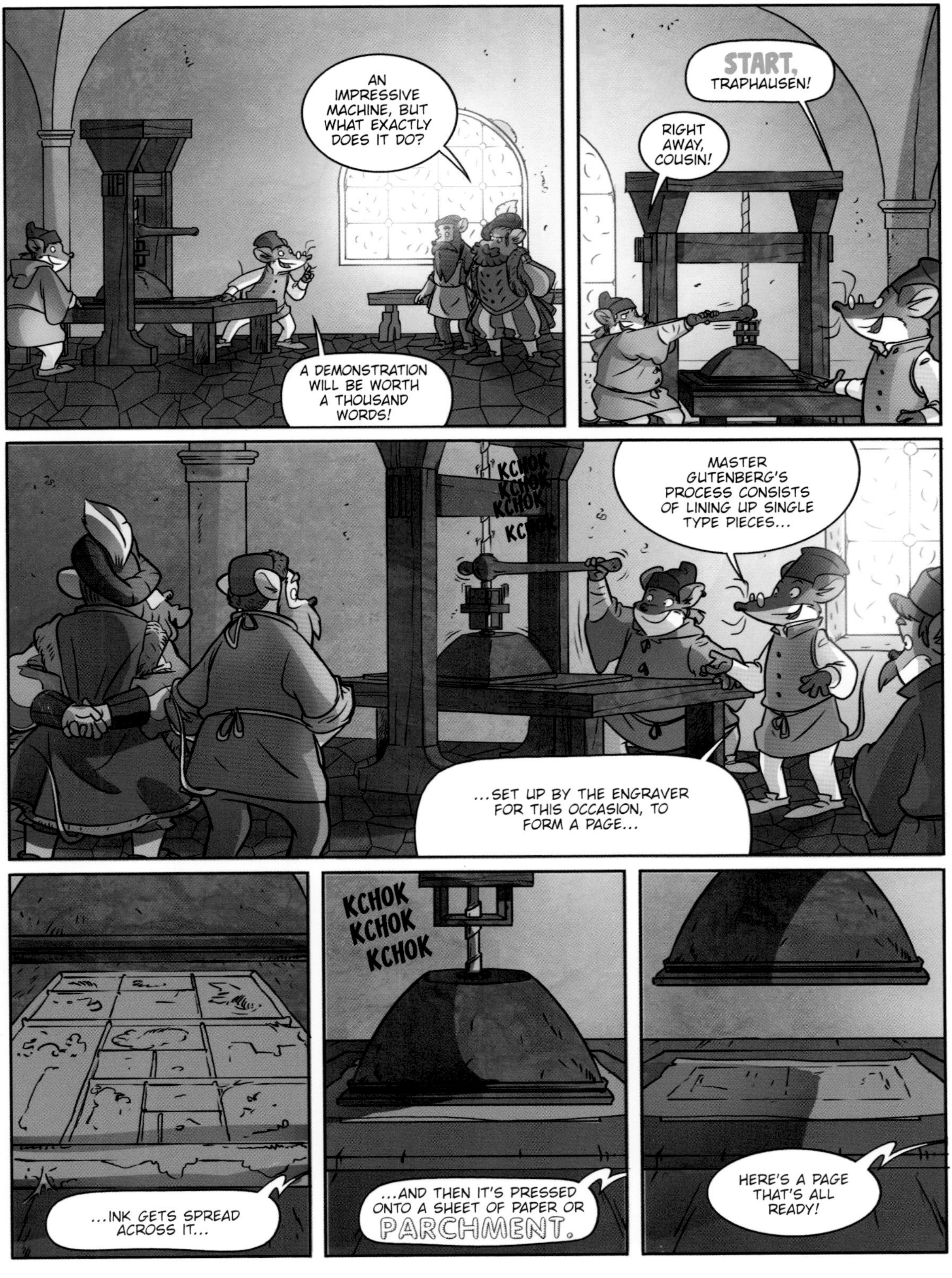

AN IMPRESSIVE MACHINE, BUT WHAT EXACTLY DOES IT DO?
A DEMONSTRATION WILL BE WORTH A THOUSAND WORDS!
START, TRAPHAUSEN!
RIGHT AWAY, COUSIN!
KCHOK KCHOK KCHOK KCHOK
MASTER GUTENBERG'S PROCESS CONSISTS OF LINING UP SINGLE TYPE PIECES...
...SET UP BY THE ENGRAVER FOR THIS OCCASION, TO FORM A PAGE...
...INK GETS SPREAD ACROSS IT...
KCHOK KCHOK KCHOK
...AND THEN IT'S PRESSED ONTO A SHEET OF PAPER OR PARCHMENT.
HERE'S A PAGE THAT'S ALL READY!

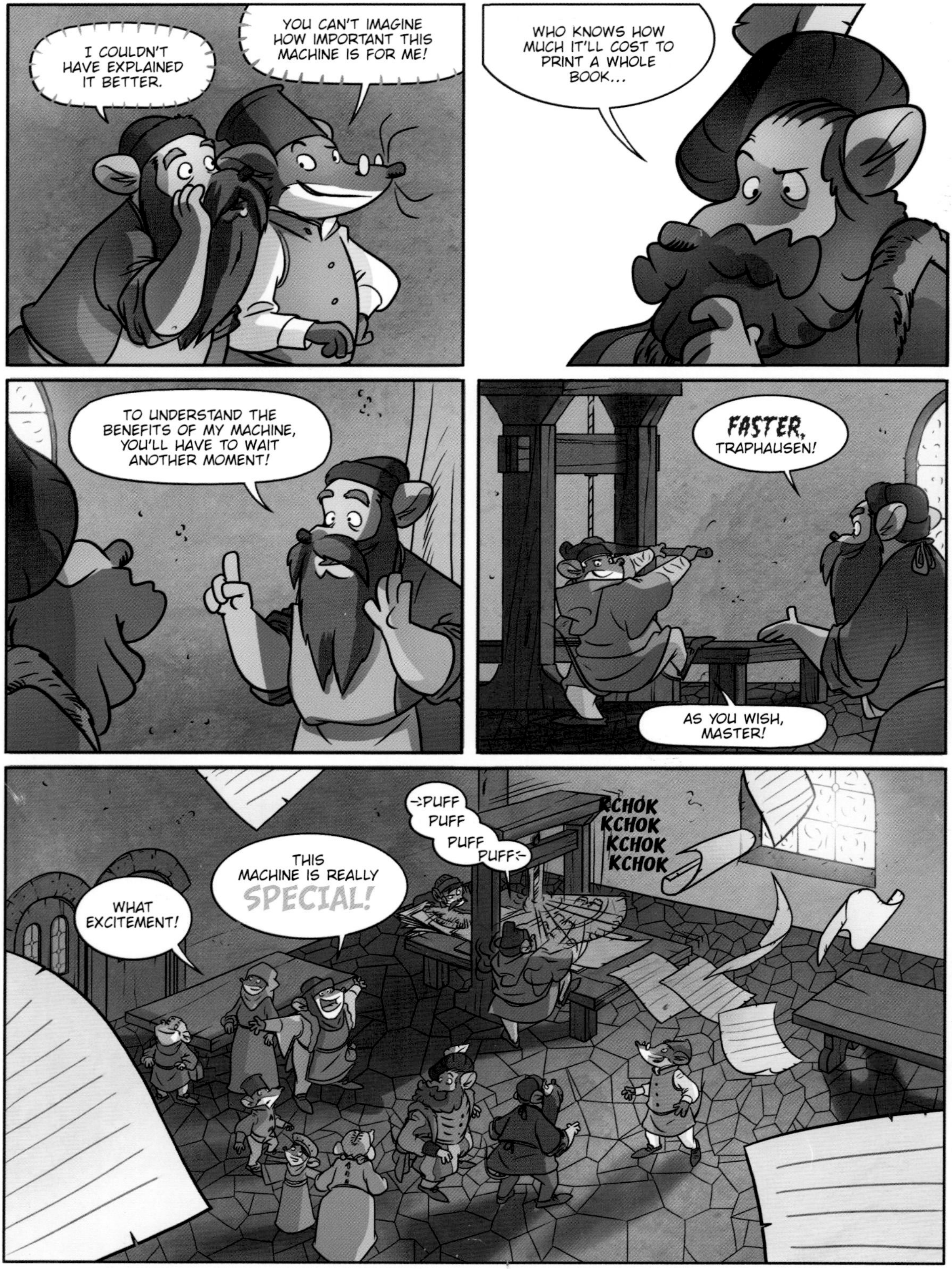
I COULDN'T HAVE EXPLAINED IT BETTER.
YOU CAN'T IMAGINE HOW IMPORTANT THIS MACHINE IS FOR ME!
WHO KNOWS HOW MUCH IT'LL COST TO PRINT A WHOLE BOOK...
TO UNDERSTAND THE BENEFITS OF MY MACHINE, YOU'LL HAVE TO WAIT ANOTHER MOMENT!
FASTER, TRAPHAUSEN!
AS YOU WISH, MASTER!
WHAT EXCITEMENT!
THIS MACHINE IS REALLY SPECIAL!
PUFF PUFF PUFF PUFF
KCHOK KCHOK KCHOK KCHOK

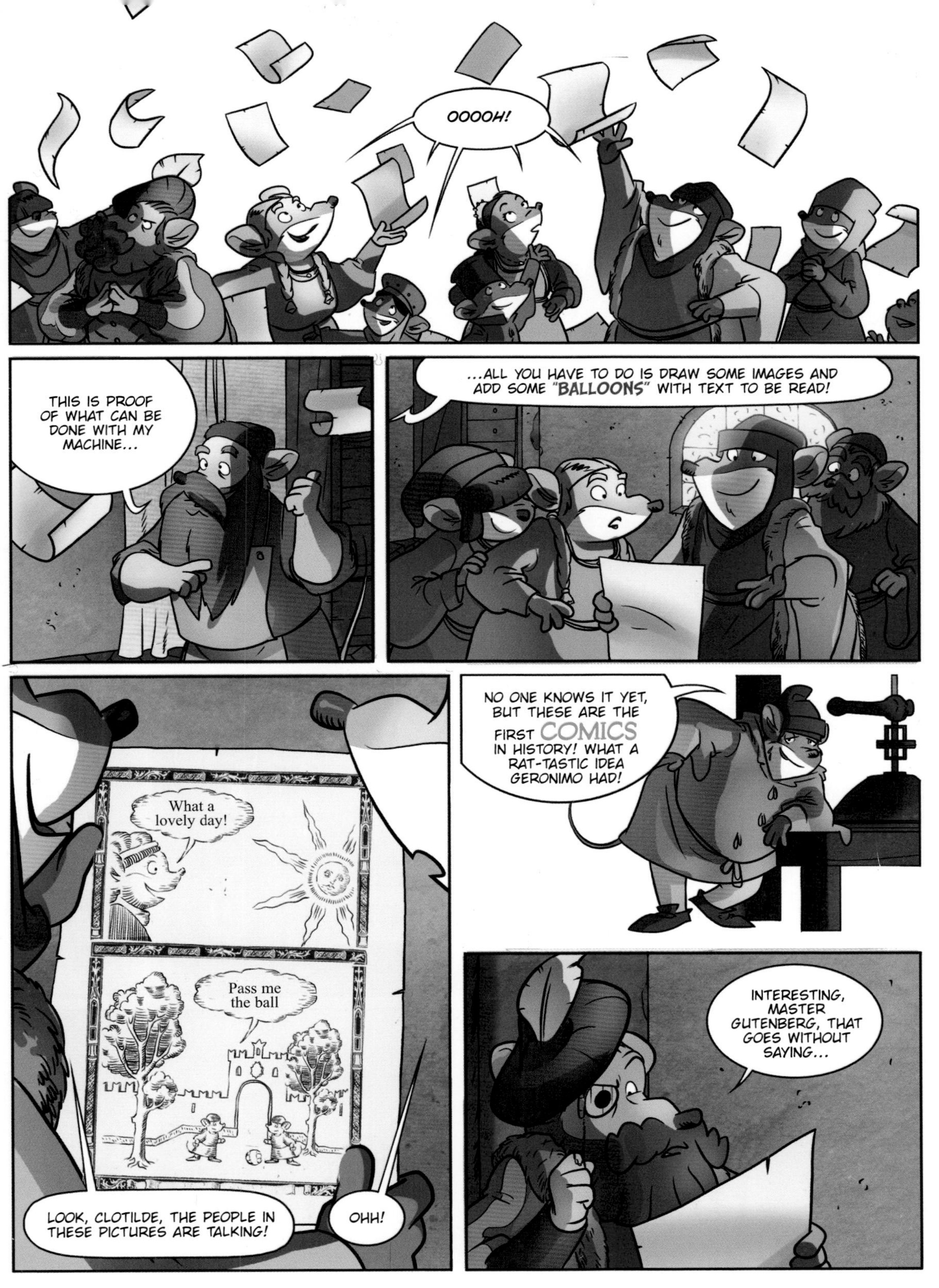
OOOOH!
THIS IS PROOF OF WHAT CAN BE DONE WITH MY MACHINE...
...ALL YOU HAVE TO DO IS DRAW SOME IMAGES AND ADD SOME "BALLOONS" WITH TEXT TO BE READ!
What a lovely day!
Pass me the ball
LOOK, CLOTILDE, THE PEOPLE IN THESE PICTURES ARE TALKING!
OHH!
NO ONE KNOWS IT YET, BUT THESE ARE THE FIRST COMICS IN HISTORY! WHAT A RAT-TASTIC IDEA GERONIMO HAD!
INTERESTING, MASTER GUTENBERG, THAT GOES WITHOUT SAYING...

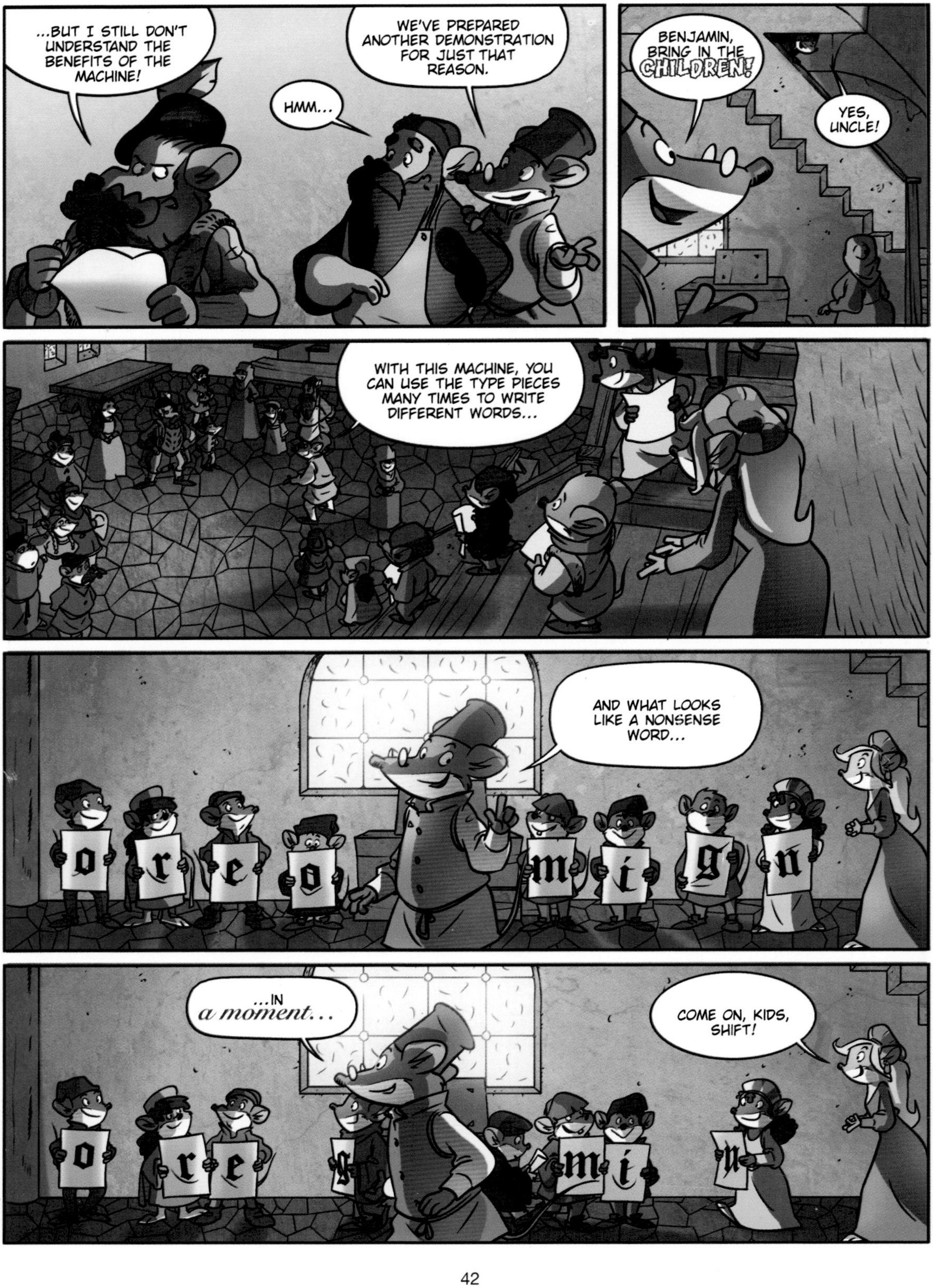
...BUT I STILL DON'T UNDERSTAND THE BENEFITS OF THE MACHINE!
HMM...
WE'VE PREPARED ANOTHER DEMONSTRATION FOR JUST THAT REASON.
BENJAMIN, BRING IN THE CHILDREN!
YES, UNCLE!
WITH THIS MACHINE, YOU CAN USE THE TYPE PIECES MANY TIMES TO WRITE DIFFERENT WORDS...
AND WHAT LOOKS LIKE A NONSENSE WORD...
o r e o m i g n
...IN a moment...
COME ON, KIDS, SHIFT!
o r e g m i n

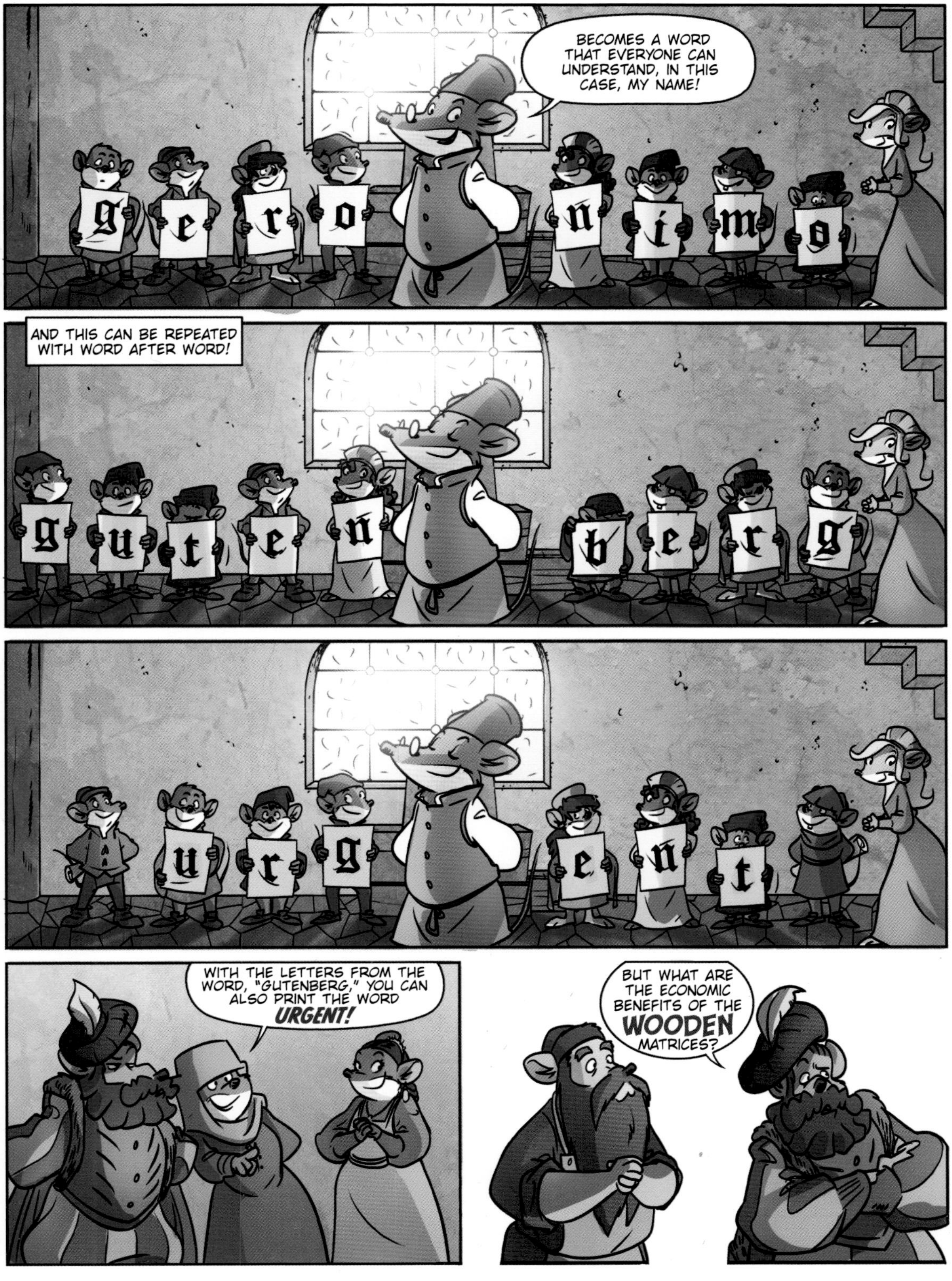
BECOMES A WORD THAT EVERYONE CAN UNDERSTAND, IN THIS CASE, MY NAME!
g e r o n i m o
AND THIS CAN BE REPEATED WITH WORD AFTER WORD!
g u t e n b e r g
u r g e n t
WITH THE LETTERS FROM THE WORD, "GUTENBERG," YOU CAN ALSO PRINT THE WORD URGENT!
BUT WHAT ARE THE ECONOMIC BENEFITS OF THE WOODEN MATRICES?

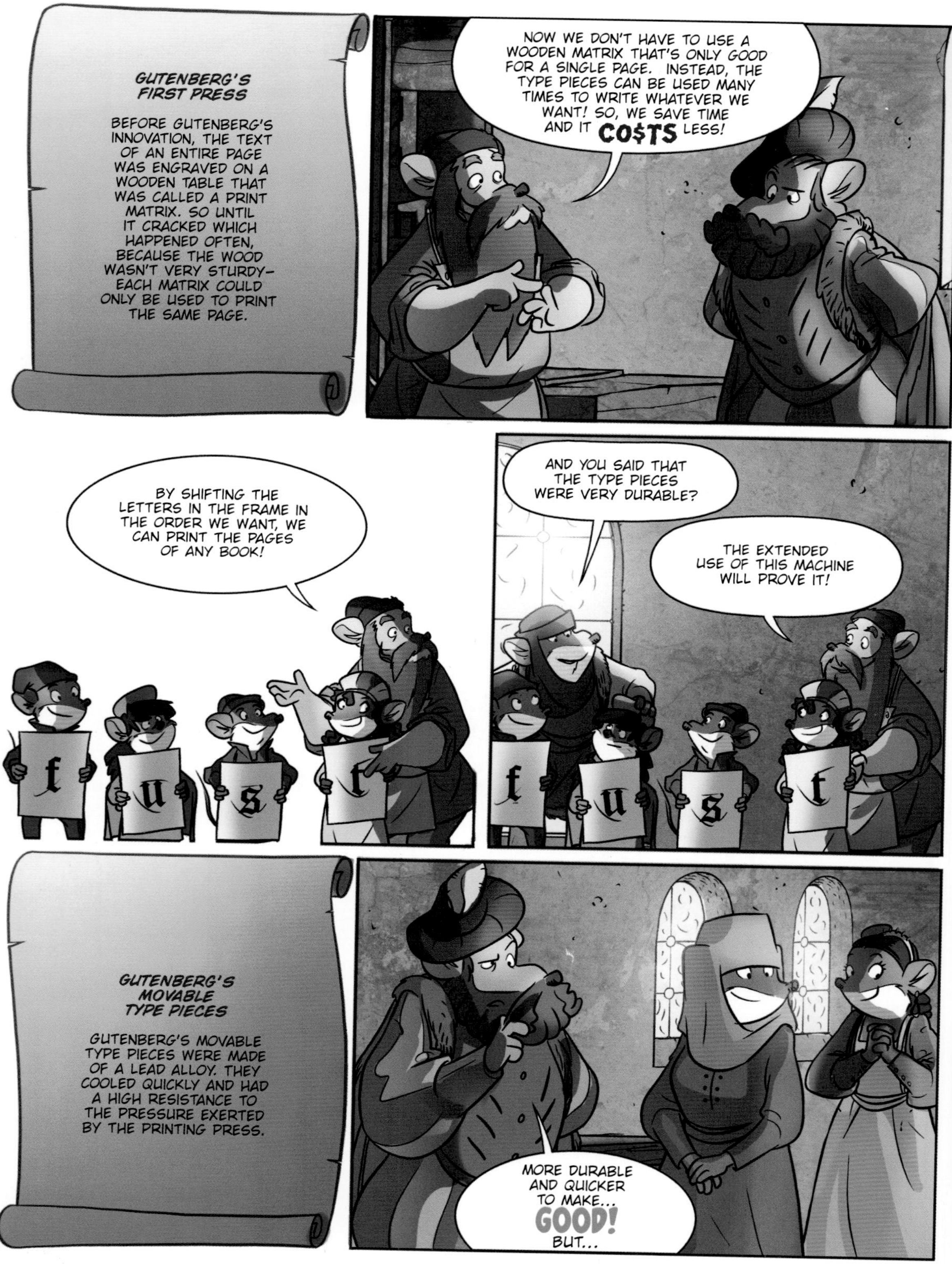
GUTENBERG'S FIRST PRESS
BEFORE GUTENBERG'S INNOVATION, THE TEXT OF AN ENTIRE PAGE WAS ENGRAVED ON A WOODEN TABLE THAT WAS CALLED A PRINT MATRIX. SO UNTIL IT CRACKED WHICH HAPPENED OFTEN, BECAUSE THE WOOD WASN'T VERY STURDY—EACH MATRIX COULD ONLY BE USED TO PRINT THE SAME PAGE.
NOW WE DON'T HAVE TO USE A WOODEN MATRIX THAT'S ONLY GOOD FOR A SINGLE PAGE. INSTEAD, THE TYPE PIECES CAN BE USED MANY TIMES TO WRITE WHATEVER WE WANT! SO, WE SAVE TIME AND IT CO$TS LESS!
BY SHIFTING THE LETTERS IN THE FRAME IN THE ORDER WE WANT, WE CAN PRINT THE PAGES OF ANY BOOK!
f u s t
AND YOU SAID THAT THE TYPE PIECES WERE VERY DURABLE?
THE EXTENDED USE OF THIS MACHINE WILL PROVE IT!
f u s t
GUTENBERG'S MOVABLE TYPE PIECES
GUTENBERG'S MOVABLE TYPE PIECES WERE MADE OF A LEAD ALLOY. THEY COOLED QUICKLY AND HAD A HIGH RESISTANCE TO THE PRESSURE EXERTED BY THE PRINTING PRESS.
MORE DURABLE AND QUICKER TO MAKE... GOOD! BUT...

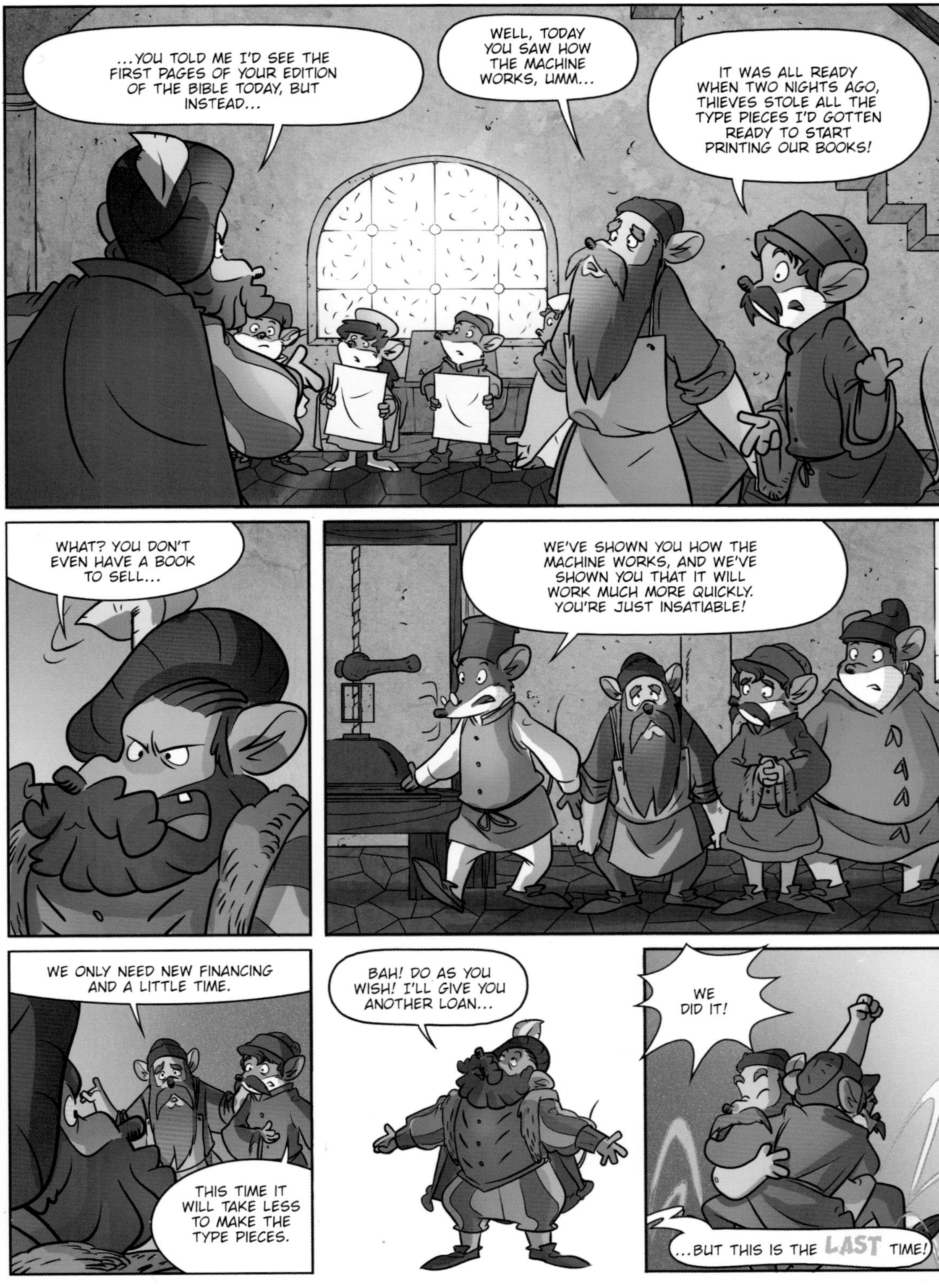
...YOU TOLD ME I'D SEE THE FIRST PAGES OF YOUR EDITION OF THE BIBLE TODAY, BUT INSTEAD...
WELL, TODAY YOU SAW HOW THE MACHINE WORKS, UMM...
IT WAS ALL READY WHEN TWO NIGHTS AGO, THIEVES STOLE ALL THE TYPE PIECES I'D GOTTEN READY TO START PRINTING OUR BOOKS!
WHAT? YOU DON'T EVEN HAVE A BOOK TO SELL...
WE'VE SHOWN YOU HOW THE MACHINE WORKS, AND WE'VE SHOWN YOU THAT IT WILL WORK MUCH MORE QUICKLY. YOU'RE JUST INSATIABLE!
WE ONLY NEED NEW FINANCING AND A LITTLE TIME.
THIS TIME IT WILL TAKE LESS TO MAKE THE TYPE PIECES.
BAH! DO AS YOU WISH! I'LL GIVE YOU ANOTHER LOAN...
WE DID IT!
...BUT THIS IS THE LAST TIME!

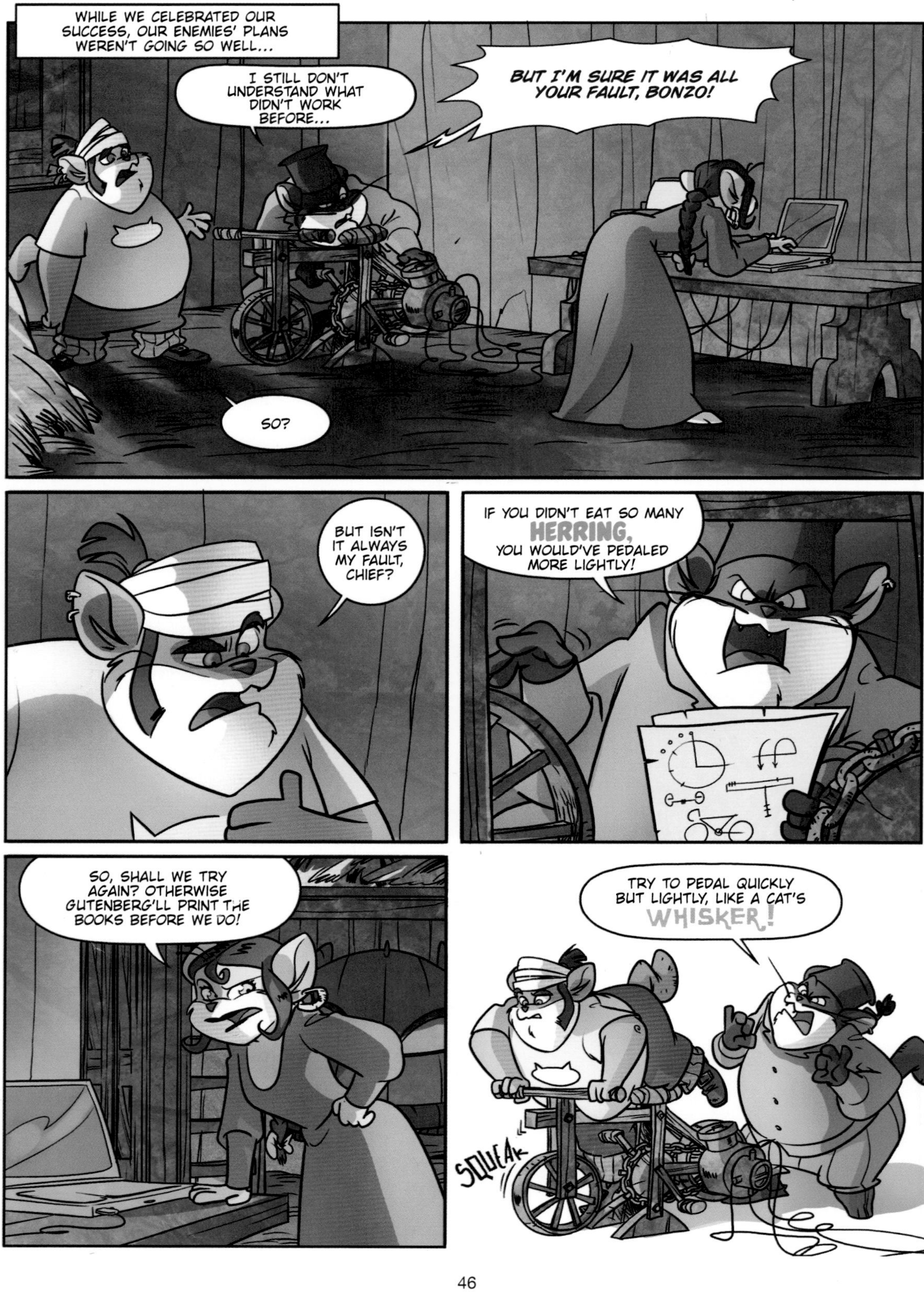
WHILE WE CELEBRATED OUR SUCCESS, OUR ENEMIES' PLANS WEREN'T GOING SO WELL...
I STILL DON'T UNDERSTAND WHAT DIDN'T WORK BEFORE...
BUT I'M SURE IT WAS ALL YOUR FAULT, BONZO!
SO?
BUT ISN'T IT ALWAYS MY FAULT, CHIEF?
IF YOU DIDN'T EAT SO MANY HERRING, YOU WOULD'VE PEDALED MORE LIGHTLY!
SO, SHALL WE TRY AGAIN? OTHERWISE GUTENBERG'LL PRINT THE BOOKS BEFORE WE DO!
TRY TO PEDAL QUICKLY BUT LIGHTLY, LIKE A CAT'S WHISKER!
SQUEAK

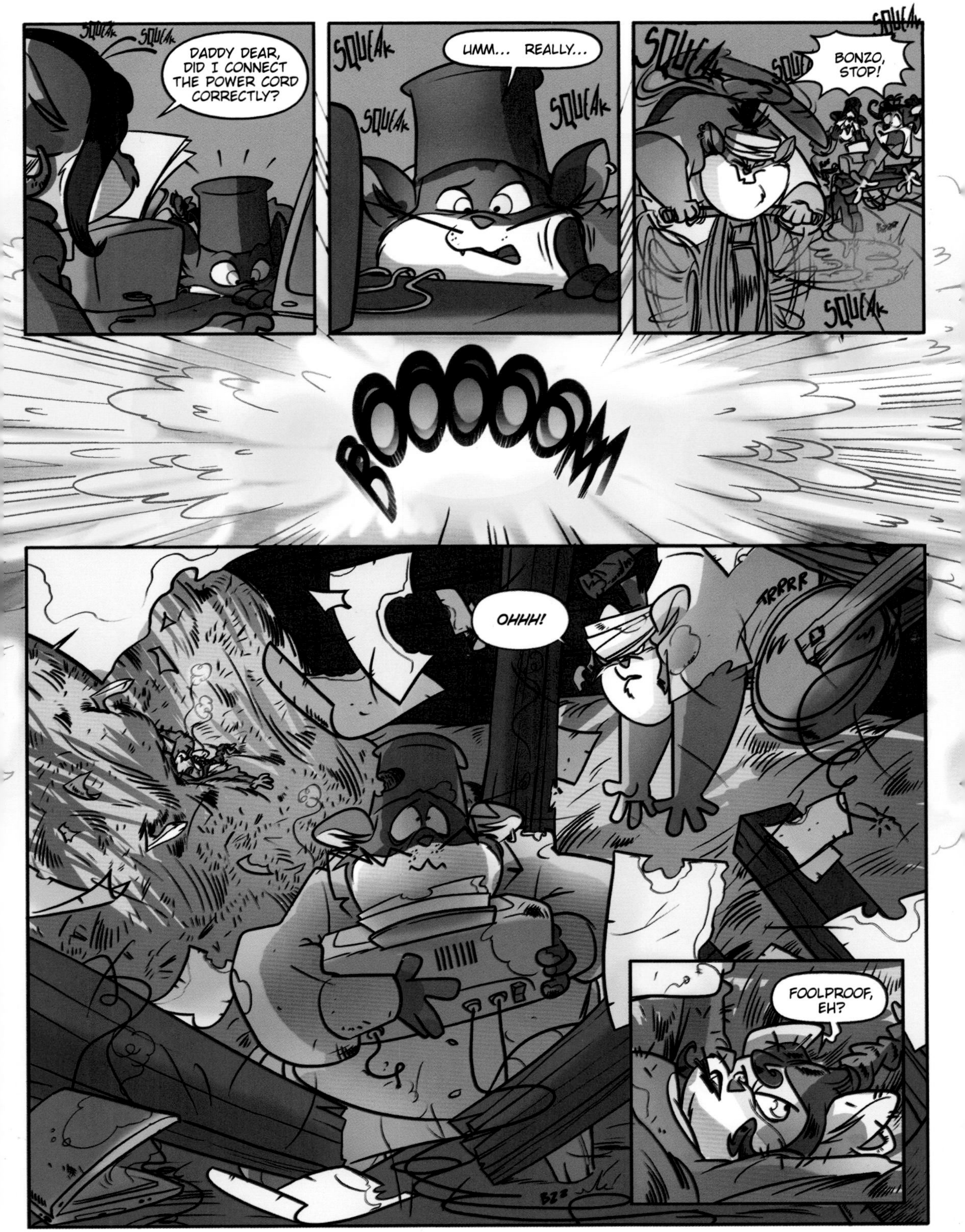
SQUEAK
SQUEAK
DADDY DEAR, DID I CONNECT THE POWER CORD CORRECTLY?
SQUEAK
UMM... REALLY...
SQUEAK
SQUEAK
SQUEAK
BONZO, STOP!
SQUEAK
BOOOOOOM
OHHH!
TRRRR
FOOLPROOF, EH?

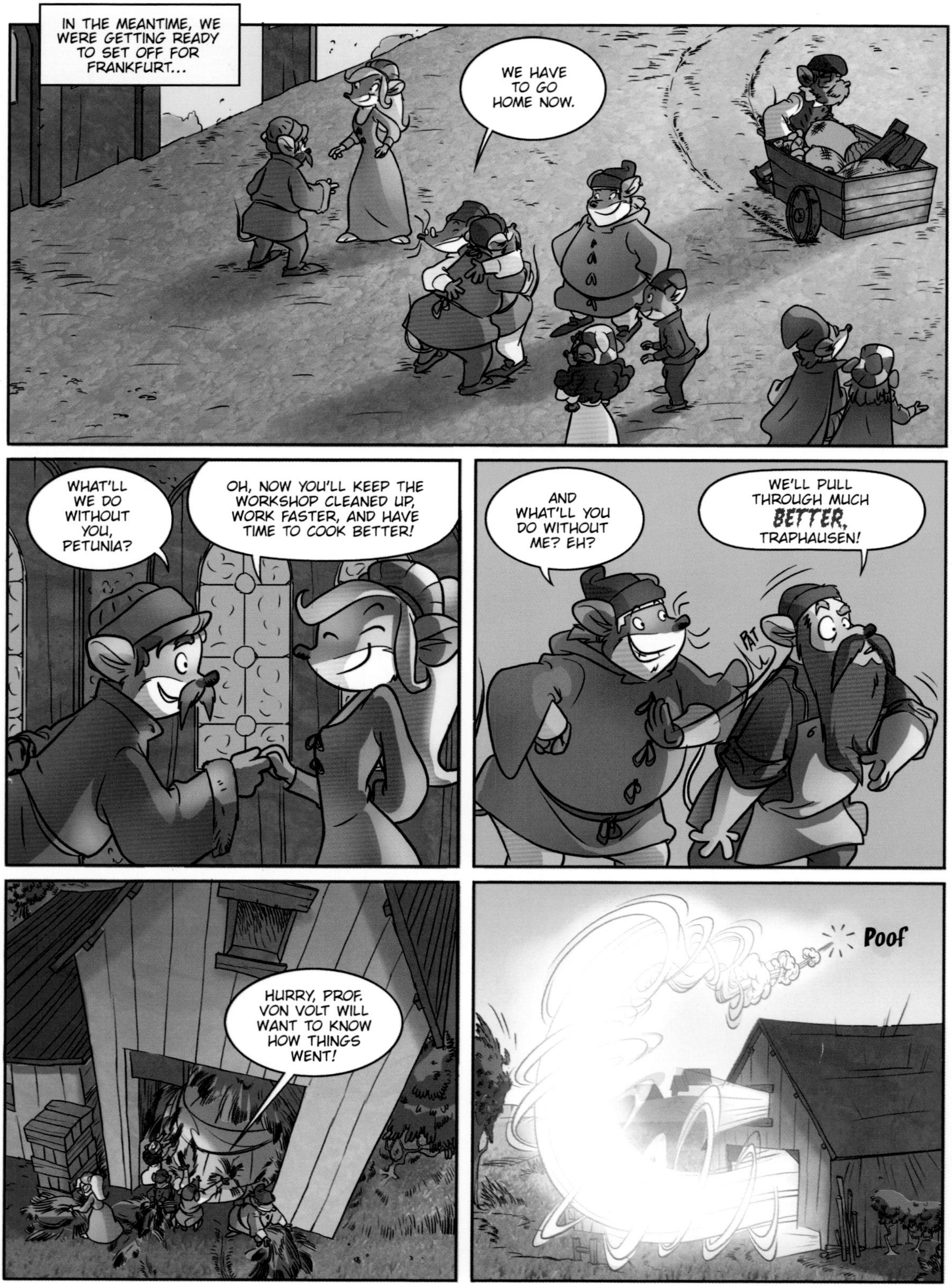

IN THE MEANTIME, WE WERE GETTING READY TO SET OFF FOR FRANKFURT...
WE HAVE TO GO HOME NOW.
WHAT'LL WE DO WITHOUT YOU, PETUNIA?
OH, NOW YOU'LL KEEP THE WORKSHOP CLEANED UP, WORK FASTER, AND HAVE TIME TO COOK BETTER!
AND WHAT'LL YOU DO WITHOUT ME? EH?
WE'LL PULL THROUGH MUCH BETTER, TRAPHAUSEN!
PAT
HURRY, PROF. VON VOLT WILL WANT TO KNOW HOW THINGS WENT!
Poof

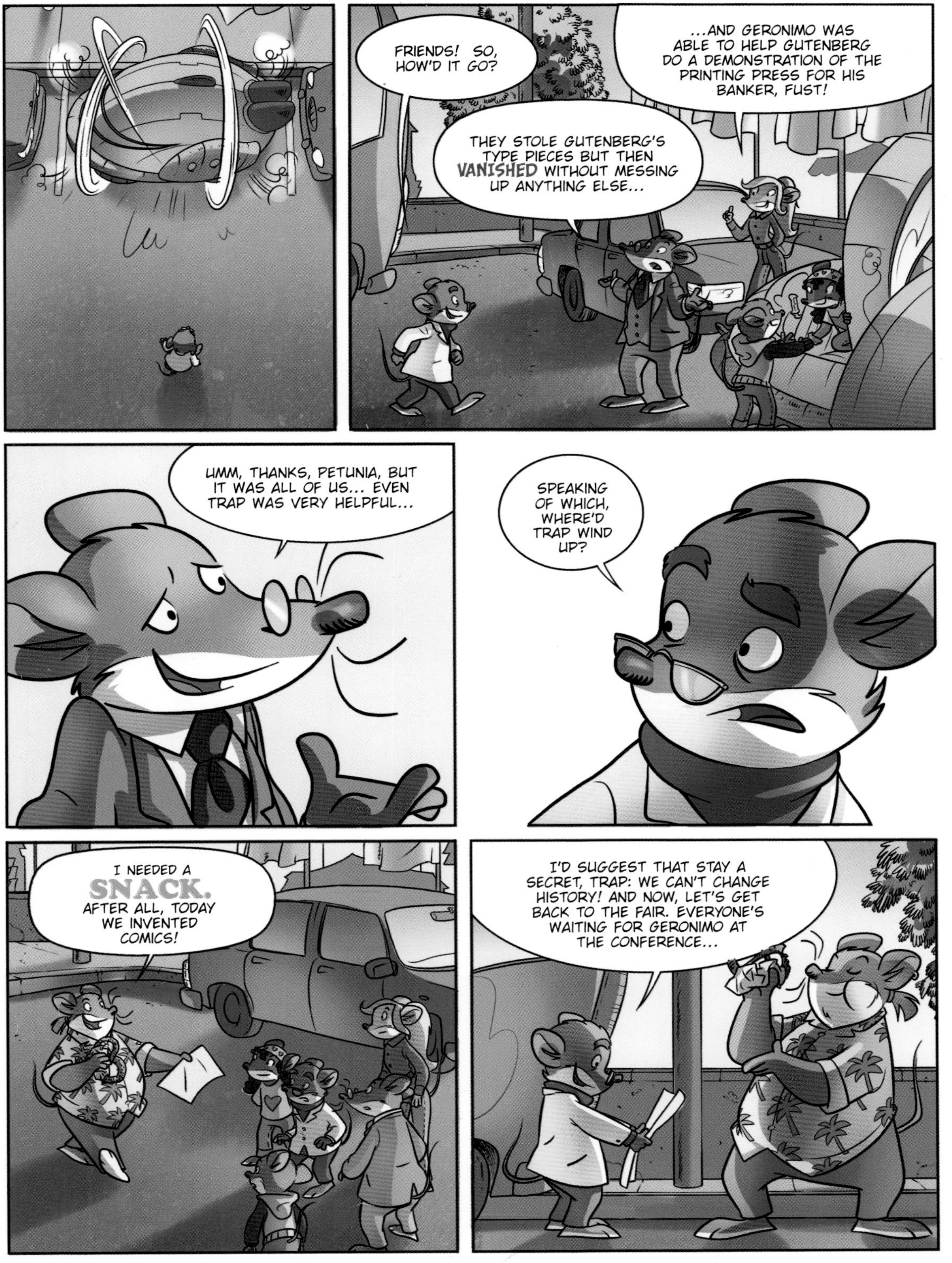
FRIENDS! SO, HOW'D IT GO?
...AND GERONIMO WAS ABLE TO HELP GUTENBERG DO A DEMONSTRATION OF THE PRINTING PRESS FOR HIS BANKER, FUST!
THEY STOLE GUTENBERG'S TYPE PIECES BUT THEN VANISHED WITHOUT MESSING UP ANYTHING ELSE...
UMM, THANKS, PETUNIA, BUT IT WAS ALL OF US... EVEN TRAP WAS VERY HELPFUL...
SPEAKING OF WHICH, WHERE'D TRAP WIND UP?
I NEEDED A SNACK. AFTER ALL, TODAY WE INVENTED COMICS!
I'D SUGGEST THAT STAY A SECRET, TRAP: WE CAN'T CHANGE HISTORY! AND NOW, LET'S GET BACK TO THE FAIR. EVERYONE'S WAITING FOR GERONIMO AT THE CONFERENCE...

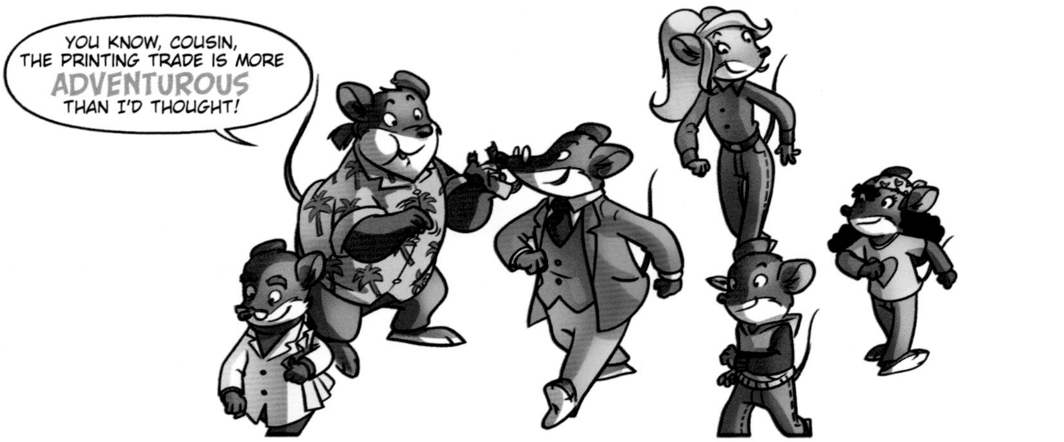
YOU KNOW, COUSIN, THE PRINTING TRADE IS MORE ADVENTUROUS THAN I'D THOUGHT!

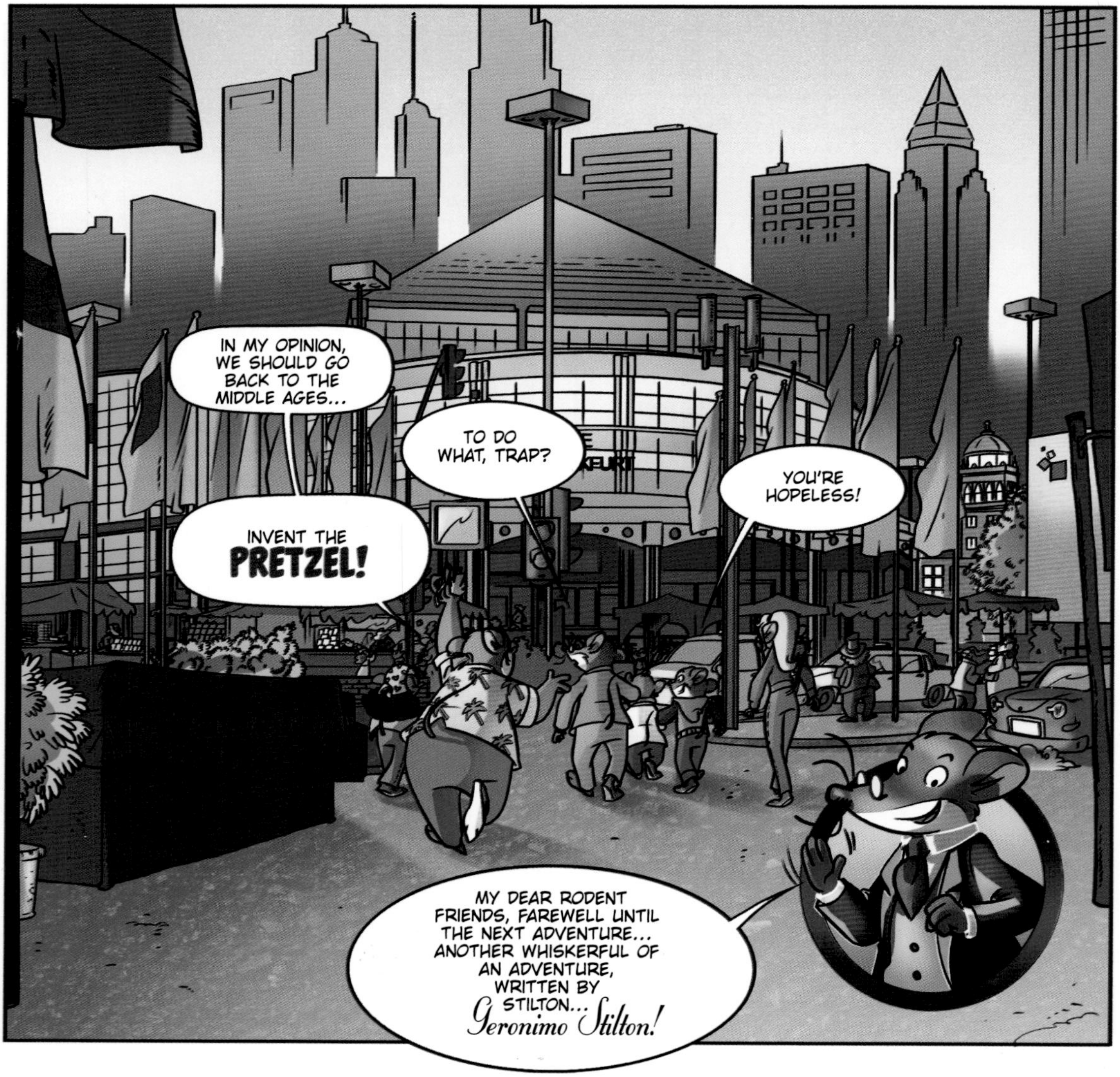
IN MY OPINION, WE SHOULD GO BACK TO THE MIDDLE AGES...
TO DO WHAT, TRAP?
INVENT THE PRETZEL!
YOU'RE HOPELESS!
MY DEAR RODENT FRIENDS, FAREWELL UNTIL THE NEXT ADVENTURE... ANOTHER WHISKERFUL OF AN ADVENTURE, WRITTEN BY STILTON... Geronimo Stilton!

Watch Out For PAPERCUTZ

Welcome to the needlessly nerdy ninth GERONIMO STILTON graphic novel from Papercutz—the folks dedicated to publishing great graphic novels for all ages. Oh, I forgot to introduce myself! I'm Salicrup, *Jim Salicrup* the Editor-in-Chief of Papercutz, and I want to thank Associate Editor Michael Petranek for writing the "Watch Out for Papercutz" column for GERONIMO STILTON #8 "Play It Again, Mozart!" As he wrote, I've been super-busy preparing such new Papercutz titles as DANCE CLASS by Béka and Crip and "Monster Mess" by Lewis Trondheim for publication. Not to mention, working on our other continuing titles, such as CLASSICS ILLUSTRATED DELUXE#7 "Around the World in 80 Days" by Jules Verne, adapted by Dauvillier and Soleihac. If you think Geronimo's journeys through time are exciting, you'll love Phileas Fogg's attempt to travel around our planet in 1872 in a mere 80 days! For a peek at each of these titles, just check out the samples on the following pages.

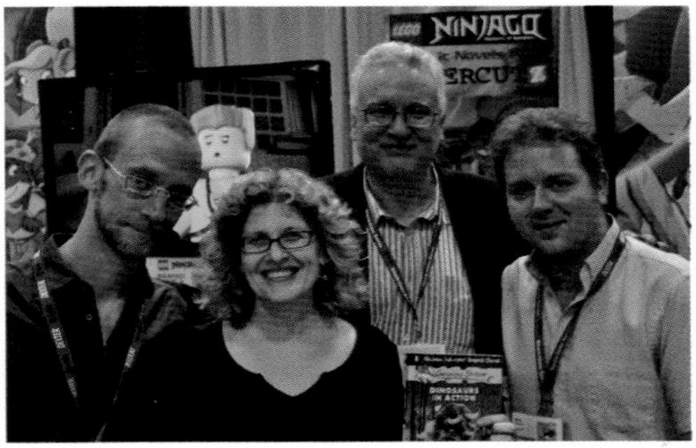
NINJAGO

Back to GERONIMO STILTON. Many of you may wonder how Geronimo has the time to write his many books, edit the Rodent's Gazette, and also write these graphic novels? Well, the truth is he has a little help. Here to explain is Michele Foschini...

I have been a comic book writer for a number of years, but I have never had more fun doing this than when I do it for Dr. Stilton, *Geronimo Stilton!* As you might know, Geronimo (don't tell him I call him that, we're not really on first name basis yet!) often has to travel back in time, courtesy of Professor Von Volt's time machine, in order to foil the Pirate Cats's many plans to turn a profit by altering history.

Every time Geronimo comes back from one such adventure, he writes a detailed account of everything that's happened for his journals, and I get to read the entries. I then summarize them in a few pages, and along with my pal and collaborator Leonardo Favia we write the story down... much like in a movie script, with scene descriptions and dialogue lines, which is how a graphic novel is written.

Then an artist comes in and illustrates the story in such rat-tastic detail that oftentimes, when I re-read our work once it's printed, I feel as if I was with Geronimo on that adventure myself!

It's a real blast writing these stories in Italy, where I live, knowing that they will be translated in many other languages. It makes me think that while Geronimo moves through time, our stories cross borders and travel great distances to reach readers all over the world!

As Michele says, he writes these graphic novel tales in Italian, and we're very fortunate to have the multi-talented Nanette McGuinness to translate them for us. Recently we all got together at the Papercutz booth at the 2011 Comic-Con International: San Diego to not only meet the many fans of GERONIMO STILTON, but to also meet each other and get together for the first time. That's (from left to right) Michele Foschini, Nanette McGuinness, Jim Salicrup, and Michael Petranek in the photo above.

So, until we meet again, this is Jim Salicrup, writing to you from the past (How does it feel to be living in the future?), telling you to watch out for Papercutz!

Thanks,

Jim

SPECIAL PREVIEW OF CLASSICS ILLUSTRATED DELUXE #7 "AROUND THE WORLD IN 80 DAYS"

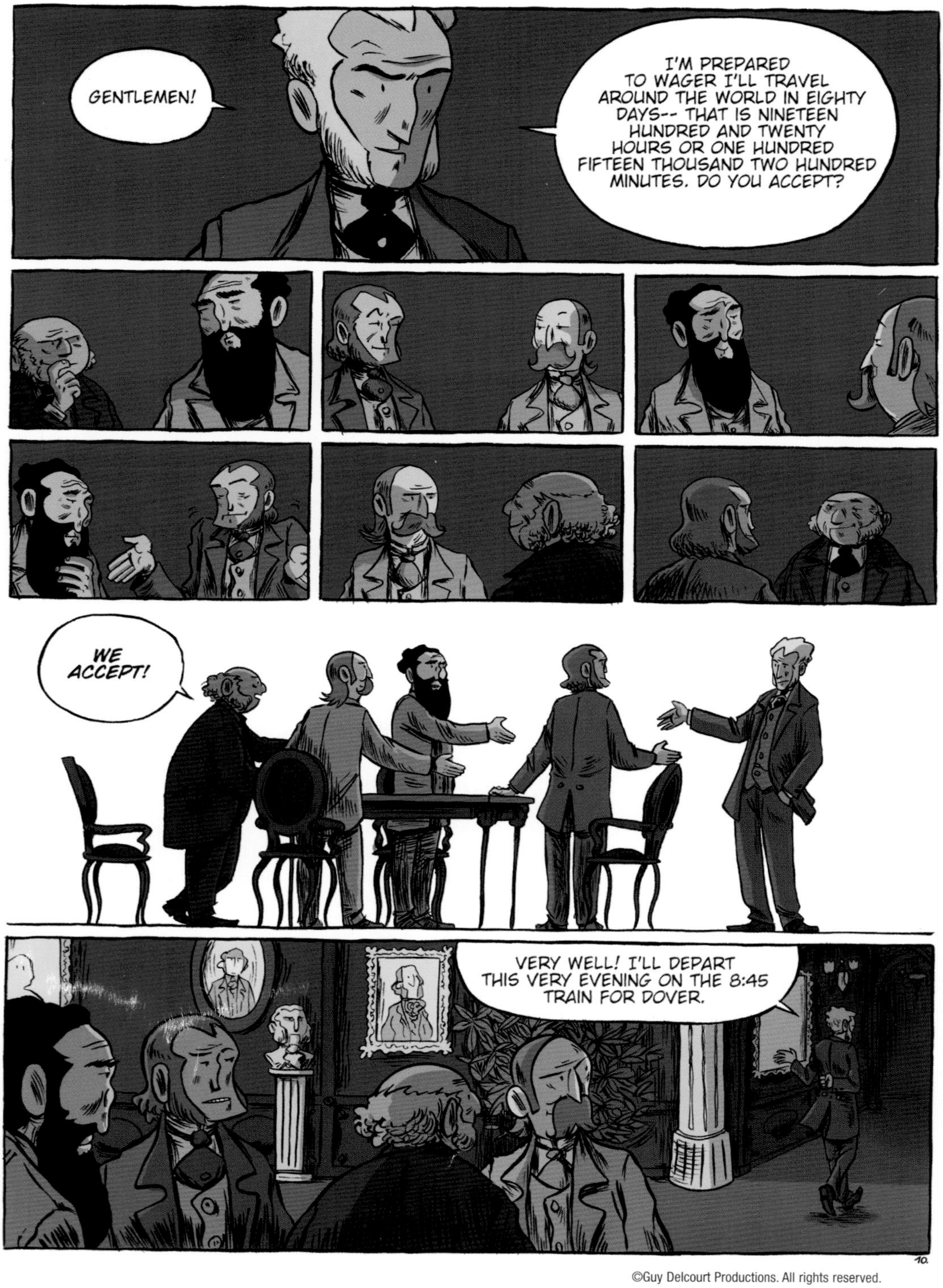
GENTLEMEN!
I'M PREPARED TO WAGER I'LL TRAVEL AROUND THE WORLD IN EIGHTY DAYS-- THAT IS NINETEEN HUNDRED AND TWENTY HOURS OR ONE HUNDRED FIFTEEN THOUSAND TWO HUNDRED MINUTES. DO YOU ACCEPT?
WE ACCEPT!
VERY WELL! I'LL DEPART THIS VERY EVENING ON THE 8:45 TRAIN FOR DOVER.
10.

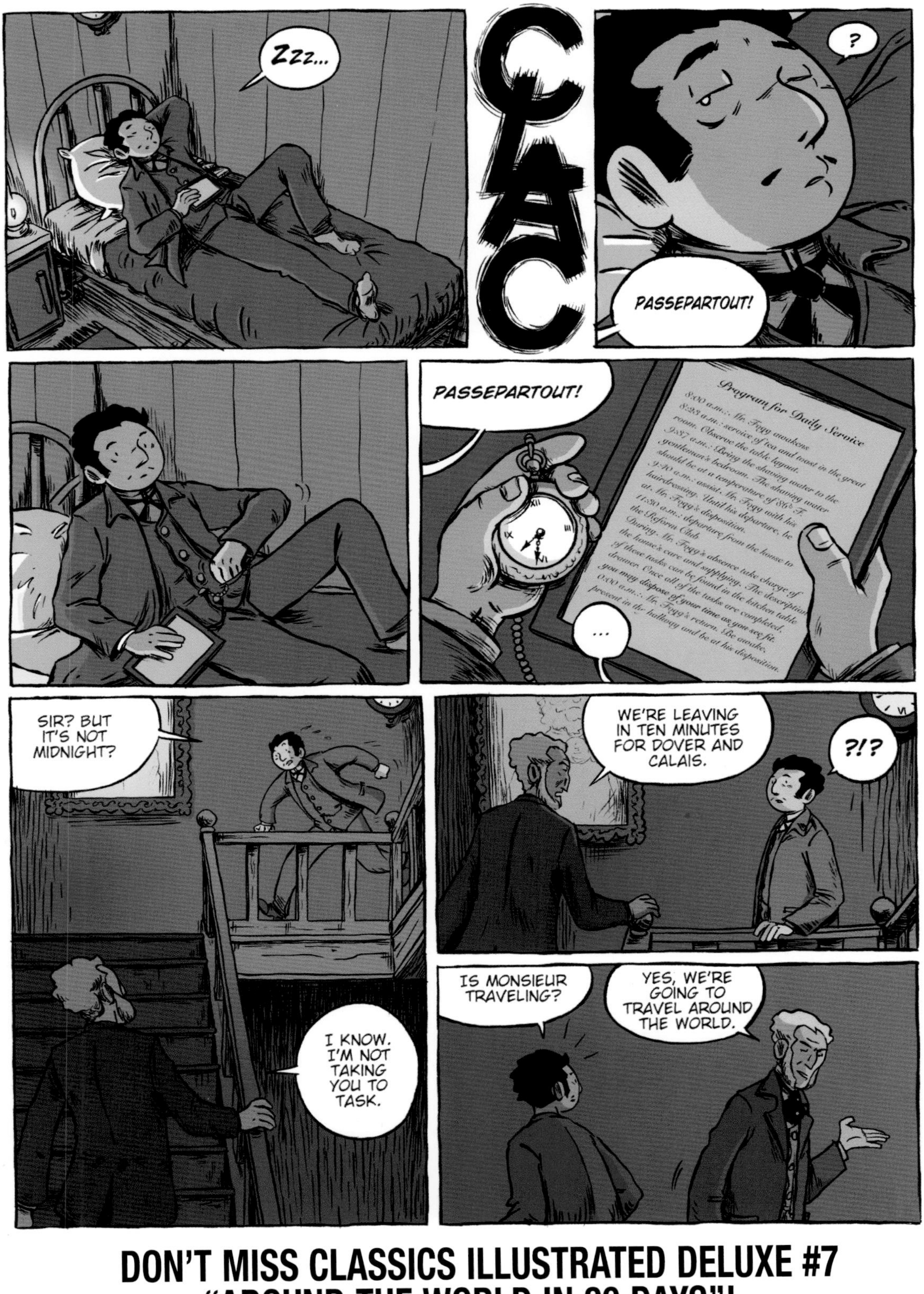
Zzz...
CLAC
?
PASSEPARTOUT!
PASSEPARTOUT!
Program for Daily Service
8:00 a.m.: Mr. Fogg awakens
8:23 a.m.: service of tea and toast in the great room. Observe the table layout.
9:37 a.m.: Bring the shaving water to the gentleman's bedroom. The shaving water should be at a temperature of 86° F.
9:40 a.m.: assist. Mr. Fogg with his hairdressing. Until his departure, be at. Mr. Fogg's disposition.
11:30 a.m.: departure from the house to the Reform Club
During. Mr. Fogg's absence take charge of the house's care and supplying. The description of these tasks can be found in the kitchen table drawer. Once all of the tasks are completed, you may dispose of your time as you see fit.
0:00 a.m.: Mr. Fogg's return. Be awake. present in the hallway and be at his disposition.
...
SIR? BUT IT'S NOT MIDNIGHT?
I KNOW. I'M NOT TAKING YOU TO TASK.
WE'RE LEAVING IN TEN MINUTES FOR DOVER AND CALAIS.
?!?
IS MONSIEUR TRAVELING?
YES, WE'RE GOING TO TRAVEL AROUND THE WORLD.

SPECIAL PREVIEW OF MONSTER #2 "MONSTER MESS"

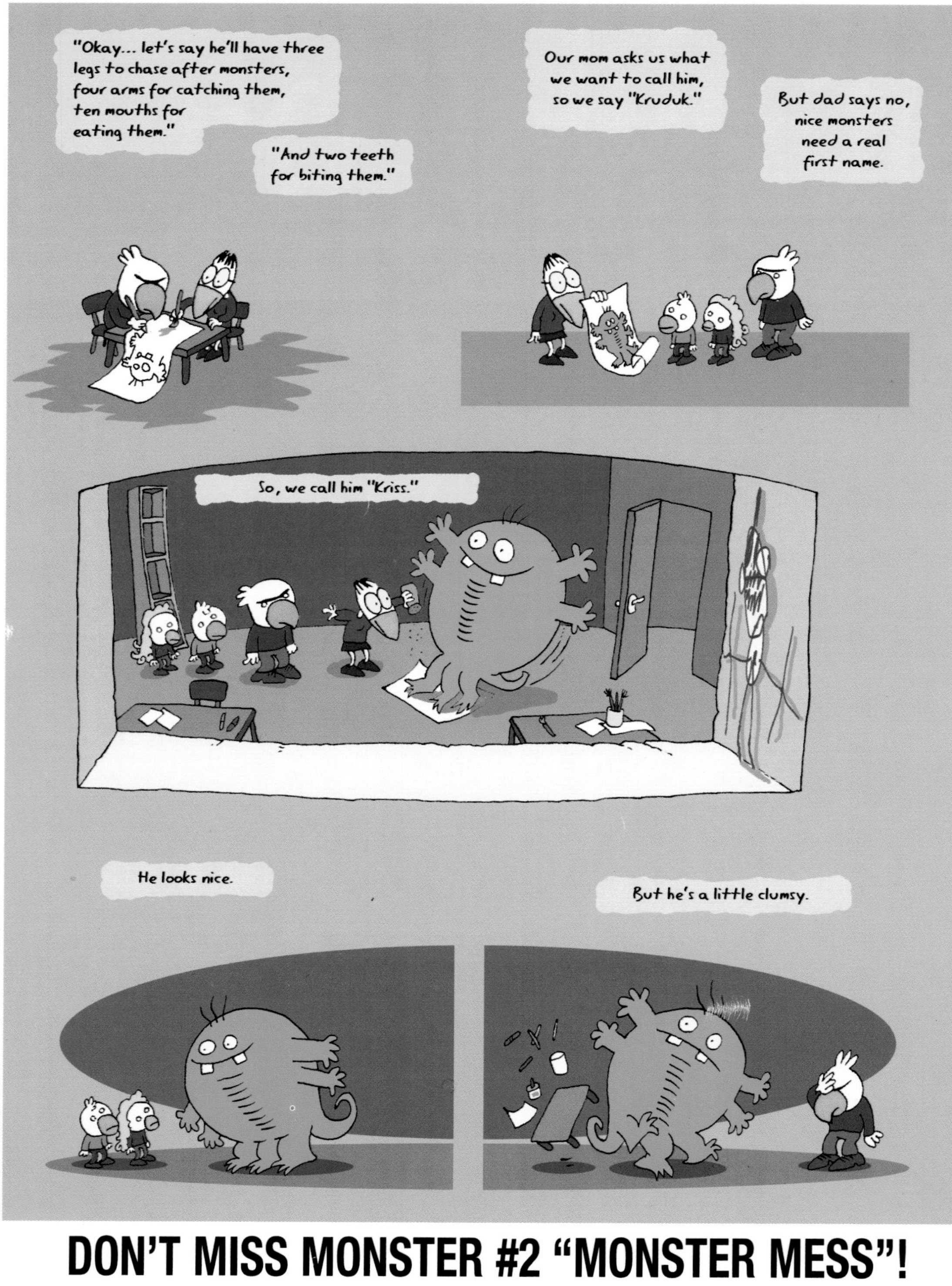
"Okay... let's say he'll have three legs to chase after monsters, four arms for catching them, ten mouths for eating them."
"And two teeth for biting them."
Our mom asks us what we want to call him, so we say "Kruduk."
But dad says no, nice monsters need a real first name.
So, we call him "Kriss."
He looks nice.
But he's a little clumsy.

DON'T MISS MONSTER #2 "MONSTER MESS"!

SPECIAL PREVIEW OF DANCE CLASS #1
"SO, YOU THINK YOU CAN HIP-HOP?"

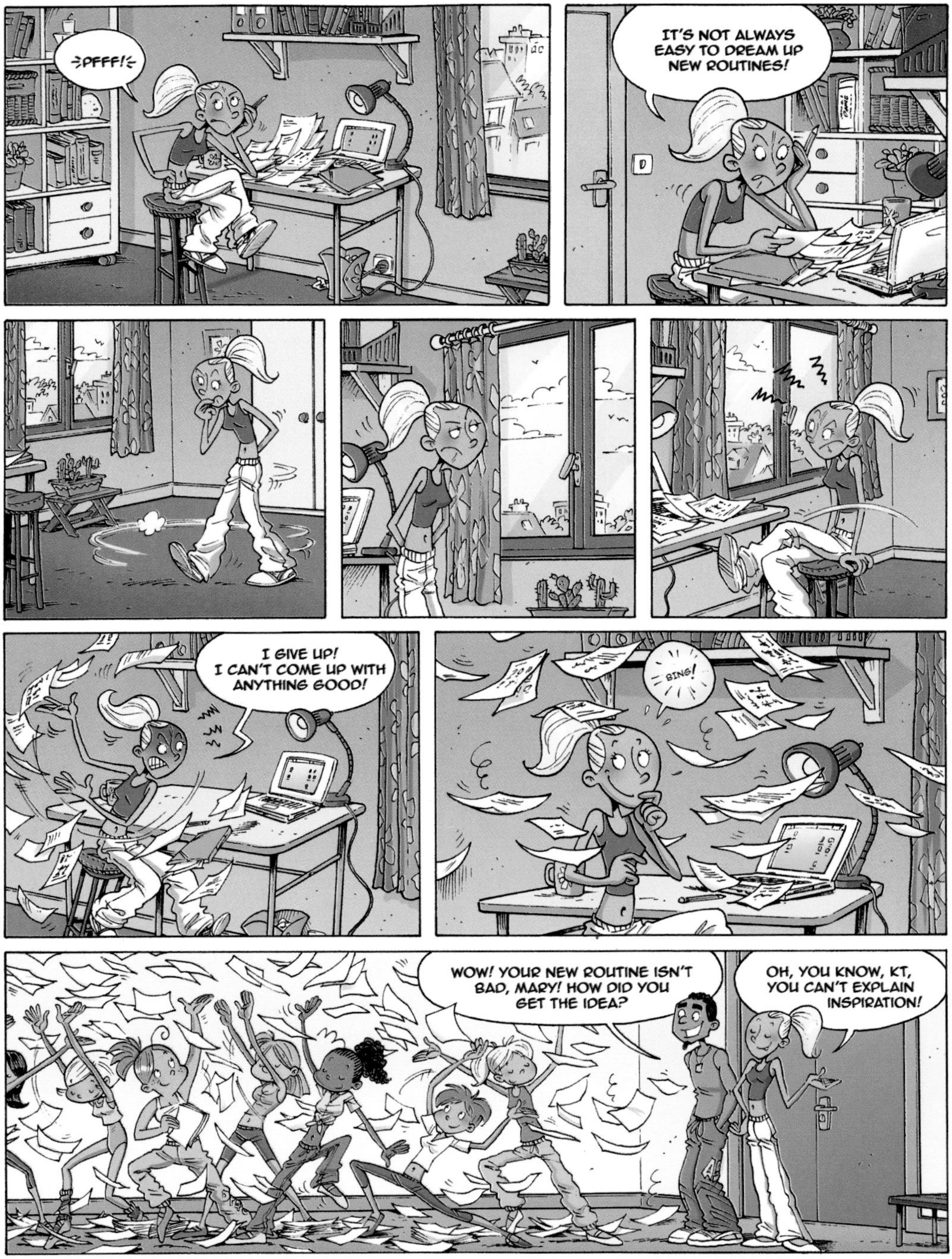
PFFF!
IT'S NOT ALWAYS EASY TO DREAM UP NEW ROUTINES!
I GIVE UP! I CAN'T COME UP WITH ANYTHING GOOD!
BING!
WOW! YOUR NEW ROUTINE ISN'T BAD, MARY! HOW DID YOU GET THE IDEA?
OH, YOU KNOW, KT, YOU CAN'T EXPLAIN INSPIRATION!

DON'T MISS DANCE CLASS #1
"SO, YOU THINK YOU CAN HIP-HOP?"

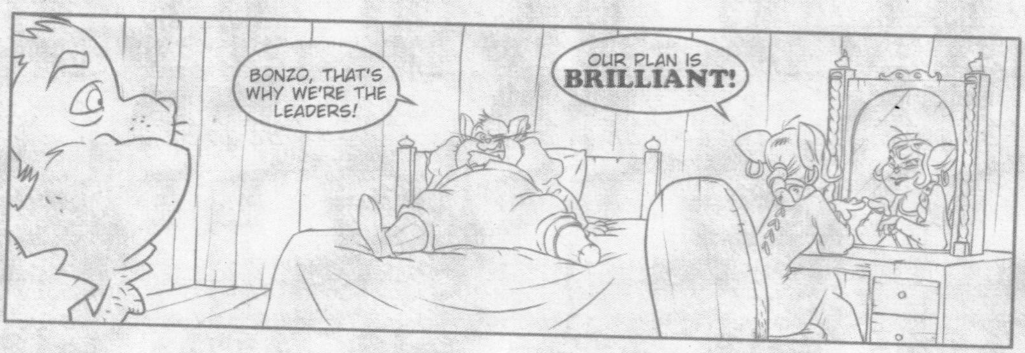
BONZO, THAT'S WHY WE'RE THE LEADERS!
OUR PLAN IS BRILLIANT!

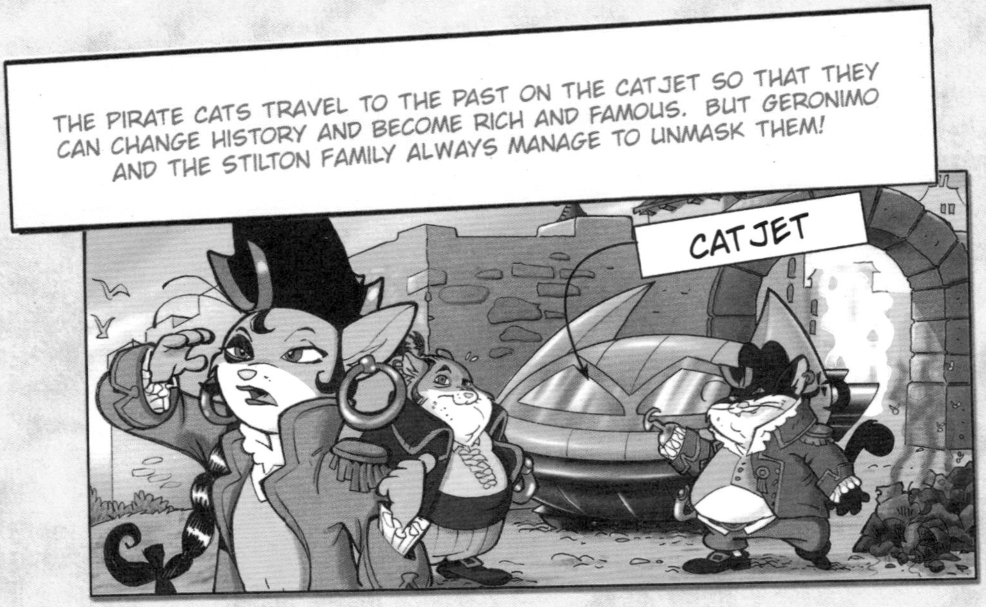
THE PIRATE CATS TRAVEL TO THE PAST ON THE CATJET SO THAT THEY CAN CHANGE HISTORY AND BECOME RICH AND FAMOUS. BUT GERONIMO AND THE STILTON FAMILY ALWAYS MANAGE TO UNMASK THEM!
CATJET

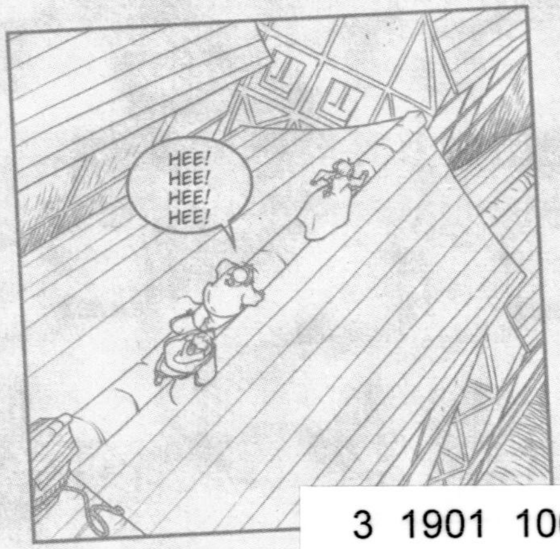
HEE! HEE! HEE! HEE!

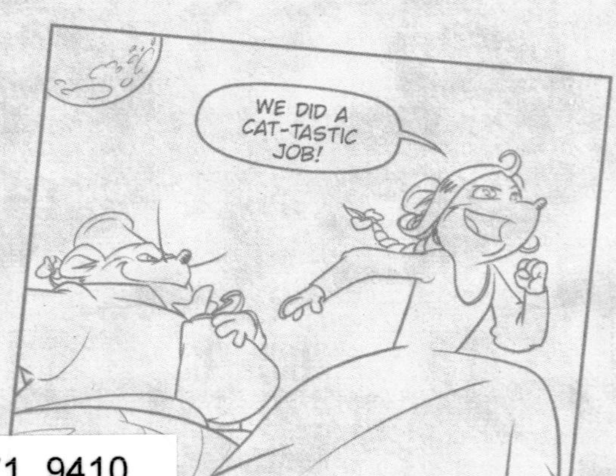
WE DID A CAT-TASTIC JOB!

CATARDONE III OF CATATONIA

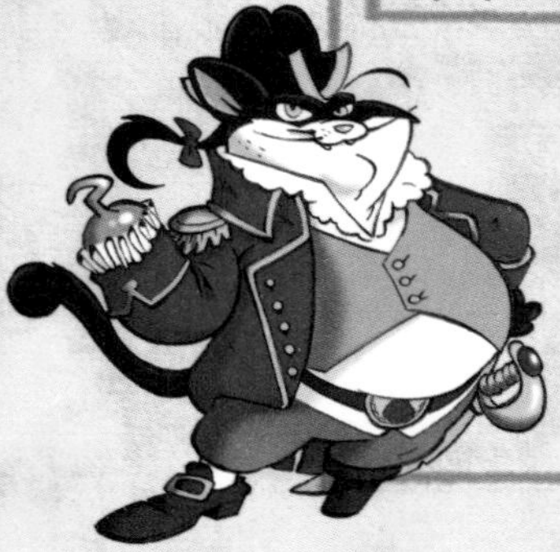

I'M CATARDONE III
OF CATATONIA,
RULER OF THE
PIRATE CATS.
MY DREAM IS
TO BECOME
THE RICHEST AND
MOST FAMOUS
CAT OF ALL
OF TIME!

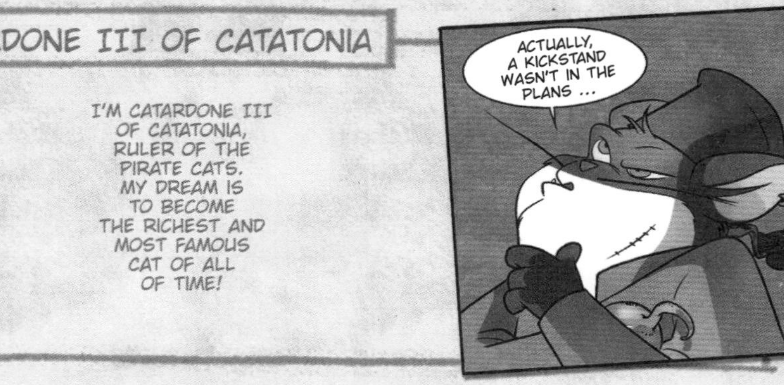
ACTUALLY, A KICKSTAND WASN'T IN THE PLANS ...

TERSILLA OF CATATONIA

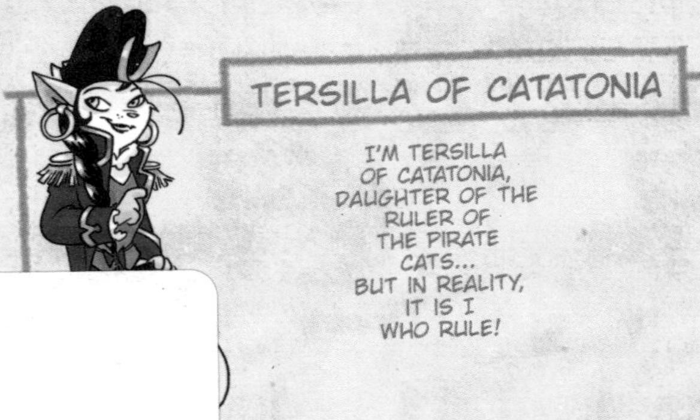

I'M TERSILLA
OF CATATONIA,
DAUGHTER OF THE
RULER OF
THE PIRATE
CATS...
BUT IN REALITY,
IT IS I
WHO RULE!

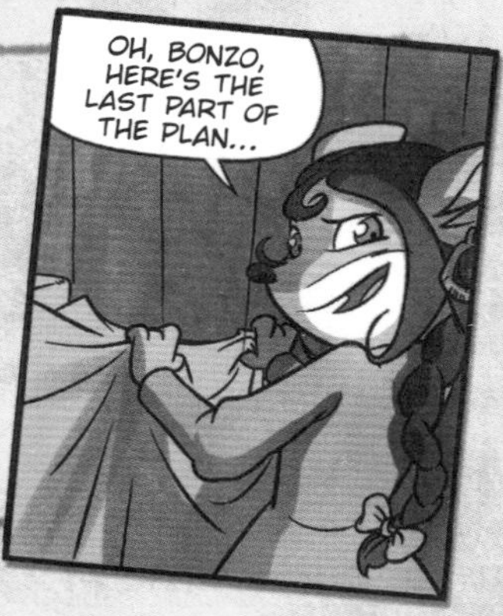
OH, BONZO, HERE'S THE LAST PART OF THE PLAN...

BONZO FELIX

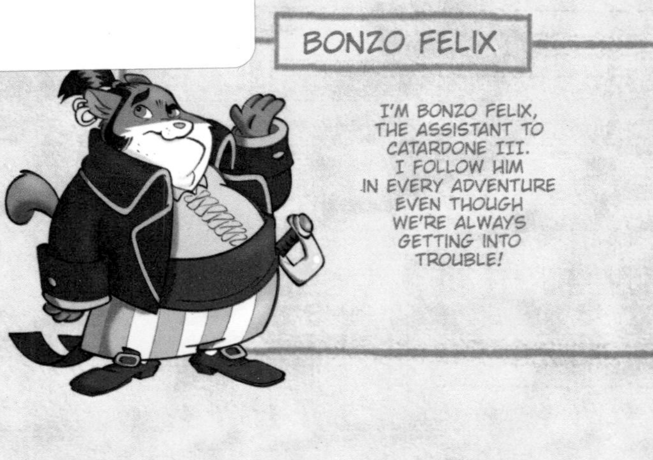

I'M BONZO FELIX,
THE ASSISTANT TO
CATARDONE III.
I FOLLOW HIM
IN EVERY ADVENTURE
EVEN THOUGH
WE'RE ALWAYS
GETTING INTO
TROUBLE!

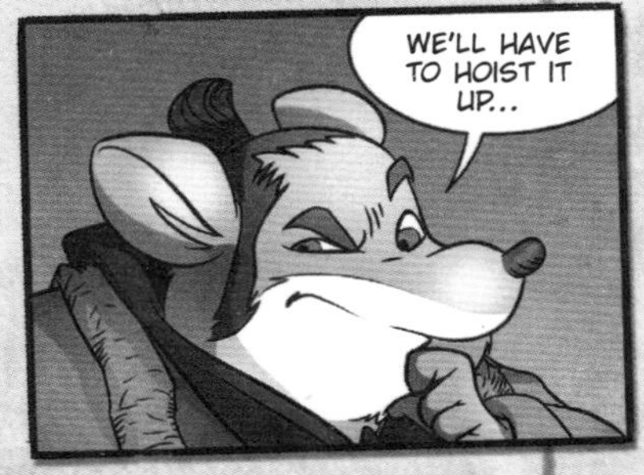
WE'LL HAVE TO HOIST IT UP...